"Each time you touch me, I want you.

"I thought, at first, that it was related to the danger I was in—a sort of side effect of the adrenaline rush, you know?" J.C. continued. "But I'm not in any danger now, and I still want you."

The woman had a mouth that was going to get them into trouble, Nik thought.

"So, I was thinking... Maybe we should give in to our mutual attraction, get it out of our systems, so we can figure out a way to find the guy who shot Father Mike." She moistened her lips. "It just seems like the logical solution."

What was he going to do? There wasn't anything logical about the way he felt about her. Nik tried to think rationally about it, but another part of him already had the answer. "Okay."

"Okay?" J.C. squeaked, suddenly seeming a little unsure of herself. "So...you believe it...won't be a mistake?"

"No." Nik angled his head and nibbled along her jaw. "This is definitely a mistake." Then he pulled her tight against him, letting her feel just how *big* a mistake it was going to be. "So we'll just have to

Blaze™

Dear Reader,

Writing about Greek brothers who are
TALL, DARK...AND DANGEROUSLY HOT
has allowed me to get to know three very special
men. Each one has his own unique allure, but if
I had to pick a favorite, it would be Nik—perhaps
because I understand a little about the pressure
and responsibility of being the oldest child.

Tough and competent, Detective Nik Angelis is
dedicated to his work and his family. When a case
involving murder, greed, feuding families and a pair
of young star-crossed lovers falls right into his lap,
Nik believes that the Fates are smiling on him. Then in
the blink of an eye the investigation is snatched out
of his hands, and instead he's assigned to guard
J. C. Riley, a little redheaded spitfire who can identify
a possible killer. The woman is too bossy, too nosy—and
she's everything he's ever wanted in a woman. He just
doesn't know it yet.

I hope that you'll have as much fun reading Nik
and J.C.'s story as I had writing it. And I hope
you'll want to continue the adventure with Theo
(*The Defender*) in August.

For more information about the Angelis brothers and
their family, including excerpts from all three books,
visit my Web site, www.carasummers.com.

Happy reading!

Cara Summers

THE COP
Cara Summers

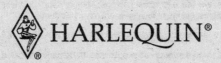

TORONTO • NEW YORK • LONDON
AMSTERDAM • PARIS • SYDNEY • HAMBURG
STOCKHOLM • ATHENS • TOKYO • MILAN • MADRID
PRAGUE • WARSAW • BUDAPEST • AUCKLAND

ISBN-13: 978-0-373-79340-2
ISBN-10:   0-373-79340-5

THE COP

www.eHarlequin.com

Printed in U.S.A.

ABOUT THE AUTHOR

Award-winning author Cara Summers believes that the Fates smiled on her when she received her first Harlequin Blaze contract. Where else would she have the fascinating challenge of creating a miniseries about three sexy and irresistible brothers? According to Cara, "Writing these stories allowed me to combine the knowledge I have of Greek food and culture (which comes from reading and talking to friends) and my firsthand experience with brothers (which comes from watching my three sons grow up). When she isn't working on her latest Harlequin Blaze novel, Cara teaches writing at Syracuse University and a community college near her home.

Books by Cara Summers

HARLEQUIN BLAZE	HARLEQUIN TEMPTATION
38—INTENT TO SEDUCE	813—OTHERWISE ENGAGED
71—GAME FOR ANYTHING	860—MOONSTRUCK
184—THE PROPOSITION	IN MANHATTAN
188—THE DARE	900—SHORT, SWEET
192—THE FAVOR	AND SEXY
239—WHEN SHE WAS BAD...	936—FLIRTING
259—TWO HOT!	WITH TEMPTATION
286—TELL ME	970—EARLY TO BED?
YOUR SECRETS...	
330—THE P.I.	

To my fellow New York Princesses—
Sarah, Emma, Julie and Janet!

Let's have another *wicked* adventure soon!

Prologue

As THE FIRST RAYS of the rising sun began to color the sky, Cassandra Angelis hurried through her garden and prepared to look into the future. Her abilities as a seer often strengthened at the time when night surrendered to day. She was banking on that because she needed all her powers this weekend.

The certainty of that thought quickened her pace as she moved along the path. The ability to "see" had always run in her family. Her great-grandmother had claimed that the power could be traced back to Apollo's priestess, the Oracle at Delphi, who had inhaled the scent of burning laurel leaves before she made her predictions. Cass couldn't testify to that, but she burned laurel leaves once in a while, just in case.

For a month, she'd known that the days surrounding the full moon would be pivotal for her family. At midnight, she'd seen that her youngest nephew, Kit, would face danger and death, and if he chose to follow his heart, he would also find the woman the Fates intended him for. A damsel in distress—the perfect match for an Angelis who was both a private investigator and a writer.

The choice would be his, of course. But Cass knew

that of her three nephews Kit would find it easiest to listen to his heart.

A sudden chill moved through her as she finally reached the pond. The Fates were going to offer someone else in her family crucial choices this weekend. She was sure of it. The only question was who?

Sinking down on a bench, she folded her hands on her lap and tried to clear her mind. Above her in one of the trees, a squirrel began to chatter. Protesting loudly, a startled bird soared into the sky. In the lull that followed, Cass focused her gaze on the smooth surface of the pond and waited.

Ever since she'd lost her husband, Demetrius, and her sister, Penelope, in a boating accident eighteen years ago, she'd always found a kind of peace whenever she sat near the pond, perhaps because she always felt closer to Demetrius here. He'd so loved the sea.

Sometimes, she even brought clients here. Still watching the surface of the water, Cass recalled the day when her Demetrius had decided to build the pond. "A Greek has to live near the water," he'd declared. His brother Spiro had insisted on stocking the pond with fish. "A Greek has to have somewhere close to fish."

She and Penelope had met Demetrius and Spiro in a sea coast village in Greece. She'd fallen in love with Demetrius at first glance, and it had been the same for Penelope and Spiro. Unable to turn their backs on what the Fates were offering, the two Angelis brothers had left their homeland for San Francisco. After Penelope and Demetrius had died, she and Spiro had moved back in with her father, and she'd raised her niece and three nephews right along with her own son, Dino.

They were all grown up now. Dino had already left the nest to join the navy. The youngest, her niece, Philly, had graduated from college in January, and eventually, they'd probably all move out of the house. Perhaps that was why she found herself feeling a bit lonely lately and missing that special connection she'd had with Demetrius.

A fish broke the surface of the water and sent ripples widening in all directions. Cass's lips curved, and she sensed Demetrius's presence as surely as if he'd sat down beside her on the bench. Almost immediately, her tension eased.

On the fading ripples, she began to see images. They were blurred at first, but at last she saw a woman's face— fair skin, green eyes and red hair. Cass felt passion, temper and a courage that she could only admire.

The sound of a gunshot shattered the quiet, the noise so real that Cass jumped. More ripples blurred the picture she'd seen, and another one appeared. The red- headed woman was running and the man at her side was…

Cass leaned closer to the water, until she could finally recognize her nephew, Nik, who was a detective in the San Francisco Police Department. Another shot ripped through the silence and this time, water erupted so violently that it cascaded over the rocks lining the edge of the pond.

Cass's stomach clenched in fear as she sensed the meaning in the images. For the next seventy-two hours Nik's job would be to keep the woman at his side alive. And she wouldn't be an easy woman to handle. Brave and impulsive, the redhead had a mind of her own.

From what she'd observed, Nik liked his women tall, blond and easy to manage. He satisfied his love of adventure on his job. The more Cass considered it, the more she thought that Nik needed a woman who would challenge him. Yes. Cass nodded to herself. The fiery redhead might do very well for her nephew.

Suddenly, the water in the pond turned red as blood. Greed, envy and death surrounded Nik and the woman on all sides. But Cass also felt passion, generosity and love. Would those be enough to protect Nik and the woman the Fates had chosen for him?

1

THE ANGRY SHOUTS began just as J.C. Riley was finessing the bride into the spun sugar gazebo on the top of the wedding cake. Startled by the raised voices, she dropped the figurine, then watched in horror as it ricocheted off a pink butter-cream rose and nose-dived to the floor.

Dammit! She'd spent five full minutes fashioning that rose. Not only was the flower ruined, but the little plastic bride now wore a pink veil. As she stooped to pick it up, the shouting grew louder and J.C. heard a loud thump. Years of experience growing up with four brothers told her that it was the sound of a body crashing into a wall.

A door slammed. More thumping followed, punctuated by muffled grunts.

Maybe she ought to think about rescuing the real bride. Striding to the door of the rectory dining room, she peered down the hall to the covered walkway that connected Father Mike's residence to St. Peter's Church. The door to the church sacristy was shut. Strange—it had been open when she'd brought the cake in from her van.

So far, the whole wedding had been strange. Father Mike had ordered cake and champagne for five people—the bride and groom, two witnesses and himself. That made it the smallest wedding that J.C. had catered at St. Peter's, and the first one where she'd yet to meet either the bride or the groom. Father Mike hadn't even given her their last names. He'd called them by their first names only once—Juliana and Paulo. Then he'd seemed upset that he'd let the names slip and had asked her not to mention them. A very secret wedding, he'd explained. If word got out, there could be…consequences.

Maybe that was what was going on now in the sacristy—consequences. She glanced back at the table she'd just finished arranging. The cake—now minus a rose and a bride—was in the center. An arrangement of white flowers flanked it on one side, along with linen napkins, crystal plates and silver forks. At the other end, candlelight flickered off of a silver bucket and champagne flutes. Scattered along the whole length of the table were little bowls of sugar-coated almonds.

Moving to them, J.C. popped an almond into her mouth. She'd made them, adding a chocolate layer just to please herself. She always got so hungry when she was nervous.

Thump. Crash.

None of her business. Besides, she had to get the plastic bride into the gazebo. She figured Father Mike had been talked into marrying a pair of minor celebrities. With all the reality and become-a-star TV shows, fifteen-minutes-of-fame people were popping up all over the place. Father Mike had become a minor celebrity himself. A few months back the Sunday paper had run a feature article on the hip priest who'd turned St.

Peter's into a very popular church for young people in the area who wanted to get married. Since then, St. Peter's had become the "in" place to have your wedding—which was working out very well for her fledgling catering business.

Thump. Thump.

J.C. glanced at the door, then popped another almond into her mouth. The extreme secrecy of tonight's wedding reminded her a bit of Romeo and Juliet. So did the continuing sounds of a fight in the sacristy. Hadn't it been a stupid fight that had spun events out of control for Shakespeare's lovers?

Thump. Crash.

Enough. J.C. strode through the door of the dining room and down the hall. Someone had to do something, and she had more than a little experience in breaking up fights. The sacristy was a small room, about the size of a boxing ring, but it was certainly not meant to be used that way. Most of the space in the room was taken up with cupboards, the largest of which stored Father Mike's vestments. Whoever was rolling around in there on the floor ought to be ashamed of themselves. They were probably scaring the bride to death.

Stepping into the covered walkway, she picked up her pace. She'd caught a glimpse of the young bride and a woman who was probably her maid of honor when a taxi had dropped them off in the parking lot about ten minutes ago. Five minutes later, when she'd been unloading the champagne and the flutes, the groom had arrived with his driver. At least she figured the younger man was the groom and the big, burly man who'd driven the car was some kind of a chauffeur. But he'd looked more like a bodyguard.

If the happy couple *were* celebrities, J.C. hadn't recognized them. Of course, they were young, and she didn't think she was up-to-date on all the latest tween and teen idols.

The only one who'd seemed familiar was the man who'd arrived alone just moments ago. She'd figured him for the best man. He was tall and good-looking, probably in his late twenties or early thirties, and she was sure she'd seen him before.

She was halfway across the walkway that joined the rectory to the church when there was another thump and a cry. "Roman! No!"

A gunshot sounded. Another.

J.C. stopped in her tracks, her heart beating frantically in her throat.

"Get out of here! Now!" shouted another voice.

Two male voices. And the name *Roman* had jogged an elusive memory into place. The man who'd seemed familiar was Roman Oliver, whose family had been loyal supporters of her father during his last two campaigns for mayor of San Francisco. The Oliver family had also been in the news lately because of some big land deal they were competing for.

Was it Roman Oliver who'd just fired those shots? Where was the bride? And Father Mike? Grabbing her cell phone out of her pocket, she punched 911 as she raced toward the sacristy door.

"I'm at St. Peter's Church near Skylar and Bellevue," she said to the 911 operator. "There's a wedding and a fight broke out. Somebody's shooting a gun."

Through one of the open windows that ran along the choir loft on the side of the church, she saw a man running. The bridegroom.

"Shots were fired?" the operator on the other end of the line asked.

Reaching the door, J.C. pushed through it and barely kept from tripping over a body.

"Yeah." She recognized the man at her feet as the groom's driver. He was lying in a pool of blood, and he had a large, nasty-looking gun in his hand. "There's a body. I think he's…dead."

J.C. didn't catch what the operator said in reply because of the buzzing that had begun in her ears. But she did recognize Father Mike's voice coming from the altar.

"…a house of God. Put…gun away."

Dragging her gaze away from the body, J.C. hurried around it and reached the doorway to the altar in time to see a man with his back to her point his gun at the priest.

"No," she screamed. Then she did the only thing she could think of—she hurled her cell phone at the shooter.

After that everything seemed to unfold in slow motion. The cell phone hit the man in the head with a *thwack*. She saw a flash of fire, heard the explosion as the gun went off. Her ears rang as the priest fell, and the man with the gun ripped off his ski mask, pressing it against the back of his head, and turned toward her.

For an instant his eyes met hers, and all she could think of was a snake—the kind that hypnotized its prey before it struck. Then he smiled at her and raised his gun. In another second she was going to join the priest on the floor. The image galvanized J.C. into action.

Whirling out of the doorway, she pressed her back to the wall. A bullet splintered her reflection in the mirror across the room. Another bullet sliced through the door frame inches from where she stood.

She had to run. But her feet might as well have been planted in concrete. The shooter's definitely weren't. Even above the wild beating of her heart, she heard his footsteps on the marble floor coming closer and closer.

She was going to die. That certainty streamed through her, heightening each one of her senses. She could smell the scent of the gunfire and blood, see the fractured image of the approaching shooter in the broken mirror, and she felt a door handle dig into her side. The cupboard. She tried to grip the handle, but her damp fingers slid off of it. Another shot was fired from farther away. The choir loft?

The footsteps coming toward her never faltered. Any second the shooter would step into the sacristy. The door to the walkway seemed miles away. Desperate, she gripped the handle again. This time it turned and she pressed herself backward, deep into the garments hanging in the cupboard.

Then J.C. Riley began to pray.

By the pricking of my thumbs something wicked this way comes.

"Dammit!" Nik Angelis braked at yet another red light. He, along with thousands of other San Franciscans, was inching his way toward the Golden Gate Bridge to escape the city for the weekend. But it wasn't the slow-moving traffic he was cursing. It was the damn pricking in his thumbs. It was bad enough that the annoying little rhyme had been popping into his mind all day. It had started when he'd taken his morning run along Baker beach. Any day that began near the sea was a good day— when he wasn't plagued by a hint of coming disaster. But now his thumbs had actually begun to hurt.

That sucked. This was his weekend off.

Taking his hands off the steering wheel, he flexed his fingers. The sensation didn't go away. It never did simply because he wanted it to.

According to his aunt Cass, a well-known psychic in the San Francisco area, the prickling sensation he always got when something significant and usually bad was about to happen was simply an outward sign of the psychic ability he'd inherited from his mother's side of the family. From the time he'd been a child, first his mother and then his aunt had encouraged him to nurture and develop it. Instead, he'd chosen to ignore it—as much as it was possible to do that.

It was only since he'd become a cop that he'd begun to value a talent that he suspected had saved his life on more than one occasion. Anything that warned of approaching disaster was something a cop had to appreciate. But he was off duty this weekend, and the only significant thing that he wanted to happen was to beat his brothers, Kit and Theo, to his family's fishing cabin and get out in his sailboat. Oh, he'd fish, too, but his first love was to be out there on the water, capturing the wind and skimming over the waves.

Theo was already at the cabin, Nik had gotten the gloating phone call before he'd left the office. There was still a good chance that he could beat Kit there. His youngest brother was a P.I. and a writer. If he wasn't tied up with surveillance, he could be hunched over his laptop determined to meet his next deadline.

Nik let out a frustrated breath as the traffic light ahead of him turned red. A love of the sea and fishing was big in the Angelis family. Their paternal grandfather had made his living as a fisherman in Greece, and Nik figured he'd inherited his love of sailing from his maternal great-grandfather, who'd made his fortune building boats in nearby Sausalito. Even though his father had become a restaurateur, Spiro Angelis still found the time to join his sons at the cabin as often as he could. But lately Spiro was always busy at the restaurant.

After eighteen years, there was a new woman in his father's life. She was a five-star chef he had met on a recent visit to Greece and had invited to come to San Francisco to help him expand his restaurant. The result was that The Poseidon now offered fine dining on an upper level—and Spiro and Helena had somehow become rivals. Each time Helena added a new item to her menu, Spiro felt obligated to add something to *his*. His aunt Cass and his sister Philly thought that Spiro was in love with Helena and bungling it badly. So far, Nik and his brothers had stayed out of it, but drama was running high at the restaurant.

As he inched his car forward, Nik felt the pricking in his thumbs grow stronger. Not a good sign. He was Greek enough to know that he couldn't escape what fate had in store and curious enough to wonder if his premonition would prove to be work- or family-related.

He thought of his partner, Dinah McCall. She was

assigned to a stakeout this weekend—a drug dealer that they'd been watching for months. Because he was off duty, she was paired up with a rookie.

On impulse, he lifted his cell phone off his belt and punched in her number.

"If you're calling to let me know that you're sitting on the front porch of that cabin and opening your first beer, I'll get even," Dinah said. "You won't know when it will happen—next month, a year from now. Or what it will be—tacks on your chair, salt in your coffee. Or perhaps, I'll have a heart-to-heart with one of those blondes you're always dating and tell them what a long string of other Malibu Barbie-types you've left in your wake. You'll live in terror, not knowing when or how I will strike."

Nik grinned. "Empty threats. I live in terror of you already. How's the stakeout going?"

"Boring. I'm on my third crossword puzzle and my second bag of M&M's. Luckily our relief should get here soon. And you're calling because you don't think I can handle myself without you."

"Not true," Nik insisted. And it wasn't. In spite of the fact that she was barely five foot two and dressed like what his sister Philly would describe as a girly-girl, Dinah McCall was a smart and tough cop. "I'm just having one of my…feelings. So be careful."

"You be careful, too," she said, her tone suddenly serious. "Where are you calling from?"

"My car. I figure it's going to take me another hour just to get across the bridge."

"I'm hanging up. Do you happen to know how many accidents are caused every year by people talking on their cell phones? In some states, you could get a ticket for driving while talking on your cell. And if you got into an accident, you might mess up that pretty face of yours, and there would go one of my job perks."

"Nag, nag, nag." He glanced in his side-view mirror, then floored the gas pedal and cut off a taxi. The cab driver blasted his horn.

"Considering the way you drive, it's a wonder your thumbs haven't fallen off," Dinah commented.

Nik laughed. "Watch your back, Dinah."

"Same to you, partner."

He shouldn't have called her, Nik thought as he hooked the phone back on his belt. She'd worry about him now, but he'd wanted her forewarned. Dinah was the only person outside his family he'd ever told about his "gift," and she'd been with him once when one of his little premonitions had saved both of their lives.

The problem was the premonition could very well be about his family. The last time his thumbs had pricked this insistently was the weekend his cousin Dino had announced that he was going to join the naval academy and see the world. It wasn't a decision that Nik had particularly liked because he'd seen the sorrow that had come into his aunt Cass's eyes. However, he'd supported Dino because he'd seen the same look in his father's eyes when he'd announced he was going to enter the police academy.

His father had always nurtured the dream that one of his sons would follow in his footsteps in the restaurant business and take over The Poseidon one day, but it didn't look like it would pan out that way. Kit had a thriving P.I. business and a promising new career as a crime fiction writer. Theo, the middle brother, was a rising star in the San Francisco legal community. And Nik had a hunch his kid sister Philly would be following in his aunt Cass's footsteps since she seemed to have a special knack for communicating with animals.

The light changed to green and Nik inched his way through the intersection and down half a block before he had to stop. His patience, never his strong suit, wore even thinner. He was never going to get out of the city at this speed. Nik was sorely tempted to slap the light on the hood of his car and start the siren.

He was eyeing the string of cars to his left, waiting for an opportunity to cut in, when there was a blast of static from his radio.

"Attention all units. Two callers reporting shots fired at St. Peter's Church on Skylar near Bellevue. At least one man seriously injured. Ambulances have been dispatched."

The sensation in Nik's thumbs sharpened and he felt adrenaline shoot through his system. This was it. He was sure of it. Bellevue and Skylar was only about ten blocks away. He grabbed the light and slapped it on the hood of his car. Then he picked up the handset. "Detective Nik Angelis. I'll take it. I'm only a few blocks away."

"Roger. I'll send backup."

Nik turned on the siren, executed a U-turn, and pressed the gas pedal to the floor.

2

St. Peter's Church looked quiet enough when he pulled up to the corner of the intersection. No cars parked in front. No pedestrian traffic on the street. Since there was no sign of backup yet, Nik turned the corner and pulled into the parking area behind the church. Three vehicles were parked there. One was a black Mercedes sedan, another a white van with *Have an Affair with J.C.* scrawled across the side. It was the third one that had Nik frowning. He recognized both the car and the plate; it had been parked in the driveway of his aunt Cass's house often enough. It belonged to his brother's best friend, Roman Oliver.

He got out of his car, pulled out his gun and moved quickly toward a covered walkway connecting the rectory to the church. He should wait for backup to arrive, but the door to the church was open…and it was too damn quiet.

Nik spotted the body from the walkway. The tightening in his stomach eased the moment that he registered the man lying on the floor of the sacristy was too big to be Roman. Crouching, he stepped into the room and fanned his gun.

No one. The space was small and lined with cupboards. Shots had been fired all right. A mirror had been splintered and so had a doorjamb. The body at his feet was lying in a pool of blood. Keeping his gun aimed at the open door leading to the altar, he squatted down and checked for a pulse. None. The dead man was large, with the kind of build that required regular maintenance and custom-made suits. His tie was silk, his shoes expensive-looking. He was also holding a Glock in his right hand. Bodyguard or hired gun?

This wasn't going to be the only body. Nik was certain of that. Sirens sounded in the distance as he rose and moved into the doorway that opened onto the altar. Once more he fanned his gun, taking in the choir loft that ran along both the sides and the back of the church.

Nothing. Then he moved toward the body of the priest that lay behind the altar. This time he found a pulse—weak but steady. From what he could see, the blood was coming from a shoulder wound. Pulling off his shirt, he ripped it in half, then fashioned a pressure bandage. He'd just satisfied himself that he'd slowed the bleeding when the priest's hand closed over his wrist.

"Pro…tect."

Nik leaned closer. "Don't try to talk, Father. An ambulance is on the way."

"Protect…them."

The words carried only a thread of sound. "Protect who?"

"Bride," the priest breathed, tightening his grip on Nik's wrist. "Ju…liana Ol…iver."

The pricking sensation in Nik's thumbs grew very sharp. "And the groom?"

"Paulo…" the priest gasped. "Carlucci. Grave danger."

Dread formed a cold hard ball in Nik's gut. He recognized the names—and if there was ever a pair of star-crossed lovers, Juliana Oliver and Paulo Carlucci had to be it. If his memory served him correctly, Juliana was young, still in her teens, and Paulo couldn't be much more than that. Nik couldn't imagine how they'd even met. The Oliver and Carlucci families had a bitter rivalry that went back over fifty years, to a time when both families had ties to organized crime. Since then, both the Olivers and the Carluccis had become rich and influential by running legitimate businesses, but the rivalry was just as bitter as it had been three generations back. They refused to even appear in public together.

Of course, San Francisco was reaping great benefits. If the Carluccis donated a pediatric wing to a hospital, the Olivers, not to be outdone, would build a new aquarium. Recently, the feud had been freshly stoked by a lucrative land deal—a still pristine stretch of beach along the California coastline that both families had bid on. For the past week, the papers had been hinting that the Olivers had clinched the deal.

"Help…them." The priest's eyes drifted shut. "Choir…loft."

"Hang on, Father," Nik murmured.

A sudden noise from the sacristy behind him had him raising his gun and whirling. The uniform in the doorway had his gun raised, too. He was young, a rookie, Nik surmised. They'd each lowered their weapons by the time the young man's partner appeared in the doorway.

Nik spoke to the young officer. "I want you to stand in the walkway and keep everyone but EMTs out."

"There's another squad car—they're coming in through the front of the church," the older officer said.

Nik gave him a nod. "Come here. I need you to put pressure on the wound until the EMTs arrive." Once he had the officer in position, Nik rose and started off the altar. He paused when he spotted a cell phone lying on the marble floor a few feet away. Glancing over his shoulder, he said, "When the crime-scene guys arrive, tell them to bag this cell phone." Then he hurried down the aisle. Two more uniforms waited for him in the vestibule. One was kneeling over a man's body. Nik tried to ignore the sensation in his thumbs as he noted the gun in the man's hand and the twisted position of the body. Moving quickly, he squatted down and confirmed what he already knew. The man lying to the side of the circular staircase was Roman Oliver.

"Alive or dead?" Even as he asked the question, he rested his fingers lightly against Roman's throat. Relief shot through him when he detected the pulse.

"He's breathing, but unconscious," one uniform replied. "No bullet wound. But his gun's been fired. Looks like he took a bad tumble down the stairs."

"Either that or he fell over the railing," the other cop said.

Even as his mind raced, Nik managed a nod. Roman Oliver was the bride's older brother and even though he usually kept his temper under control, Nik had seen it flare on occasion. The dread in his gut grew colder. Not only had Roman been Kit's best friend since college, but he'd helped Theo out when he'd first opened his own law office. And six years ago, Roman had saved his sister Philly's life. She'd wanted to take Nik's sailboat out by herself. Roman, who'd been with them at the cabin that weekend, had been the only one to object, and he'd insisted on going with her. When the sudden squall had come up and the boat had capsized, Roman had gotten her to shore.

All the Angelises figured they owed him for that.

Pushing that thought aside, Nik forced himself to think like a cop. As the next in line to take over the Oliver business interests, he figured that Roman wouldn't have been happy about his sister's wedding. In fact, he might have done anything to prevent it.

Still crouched down, he glanced around the area. The space beneath and behind the circular staircase was shrouded in shadows, and it wasn't until his gaze swept the area a second time that he spotted the purse lying beneath the first step. Reaching into his back pocket, he pulled out plastic gloves and slipped them on. Then he lifted the purse and dumped the contents out. Neat was his first thought. In his experience most women carried an enormous amount of junk around in their purses. This one contained only a cell phone, a wallet, a day planner, a lipstick and a pen. When he flipped open the wallet, he found the driver's license in a clear plastic frame. His stomach clenched. Sadie Oliver, Roman's other sister.

Searching his memory, Nik pulled up details. If he remembered correctly, Sadie was about four years Roman's junior. He'd never met her, but there'd been a shot of all three of the Oliver siblings in the paper recently. Like her brother and sister, Sadie was tall, and she had long dark hair. She'd graduated from Harvard Law School recently and come home to work at Oliver Enterprises. So Sadie, Roman and Juliana had all been here in the church when the shooting had started. That wasn't good.

After slipping the items back into the purse, Nik rose, and drew out his gun again. He had a very bad feeling about what he was going to find in the choir loft. Signaling to one cop to follow him, he spoke to the other officer. "Don't let anyone else in except the EMTs. There's a dead man in the sacristy and the priest's been shot. Call the crime lab and tell them to get a team here ASAP."

"Yes, sir," the uniform said as he pulled out his cell.

At the top of the stairs, Nik stopped. The choir loft was empty but there was a closed door ten feet from where he was standing. He motioned the uniformed officer to one side and he took the other. As soon as they were both in position, he threw open the door and went in low, while his companion went in high.

The room was small, ten by ten, and it was empty. Except for the wedding bouquet—and the bloodstains on two walls.

J.C. WASN'T SURE how much longer she could stay hidden in the depths of the closet. Even as a child, she'd hated to wait for anything. Plus, she was absolutely starving. She always got ravenously hungry whenever she was nervous or scared. Surely the police should have arrived by now.

She thought she'd heard a siren, but that had been a while ago. And it could have been wishful thinking. She wasn't even sure how long she'd been hiding. She'd tried to say a rosary—something she hadn't done in years. How long had that taken? Five minutes? Ten? She wanted to check on Father Mike but she wouldn't do him much good if Snake Eyes was still out there.

It was too dark to check her watch. If she could just hear something… Whatever the priest's vestments were made of, they certainly blocked out sound. The police could be out there right now, and she wouldn't know it.

What J.C. did know was that her fear of the snake-eyed man was gradually being replaced by her fear of being confined in a small space. And Father Mike's closet gave new meaning to the word *confined*. She felt as if she were buried in robes and the incense lingering on them had grown cloying. Keep calm, she told herself. But she could feel her heart beating faster and faster.

As the urge to bolt began to grow, J.C. imagined Snake Eyes looking for her—searching the rectory, then returning to the sacristy. At any moment he could fling open the cupboard and start plowing through the garments. She was nothing more than a sitting duck.

Well, there was no sense in making it easy for him.

Slowly, she burrowed her way toward the front of the cupboard, holding her breath each time one vestment rubbed against another. When she reached the door, she discovered that in her rush to hide herself, she hadn't closed it completely. Pressing her face to the narrow opening, she peered through it and fear bubbled through her again.

A man stood over the body of the dead man. He had his back to her, but she knew he wasn't Snake Eyes.

This man was taller, broader. Snake Eyes's hair had been slicked back close to his head because of the ski mask. This man's dark hair was dark, curly and unruly. But she could sense just as much danger emanating from him as she had from the killer.

He was wearing a tank top that fit snugly over nearly bronze-colored skin. As he began to move slowly around the dead man, she caught her first glimpse of his face and for a moment she stared, fascinated. He reminded her of the Greek gods she'd had to study in a required mythology class. Unlike most of her peers who'd complained noisily about the class, she'd been fascinated with the stories. This man reminded her of Adonis. Of course, Adonis hadn't been a god—just the human lover of two very powerful goddesses, Persephone and Aphrodite, who'd fought over him constantly. She'd found the story intriguing, but personally, she'd yet to meet a man worth fighting another woman for.

J.C. gave herself a mental shake. This man might not be Snake Eyes, but he might very well be the man who'd fired those other shots she'd heard. He was certainly tough enough looking. His nose wasn't quite straight, and taking in the sharp slash of cheekbone and the strong line of his jaw, she thought of a warrior—the kind of man who would lead armies into war…and win. This didn't at all explain why she had the oddest urge to touch his face—to feel the planes and angles beneath her hands.

What was up with that, she thought with a frown. Warriors had never been her type.

But then when it came to men, she really hadn't had

much experience determining her type. The kind of men her dad and stepmom wanted her to date might as well be clones of each other, successful young metro males with the right kind of family backgrounds. She found them almost as boring as the temperamental prima donnas she'd met when she'd trained at the American Culinary Institute.

The man in front of her had circled the body so that he was standing with his back to her again, and she caught herself noticing the way his threadbare jeans molded his butt. Good Lord, she wanted to touch that, too.

Whoa! J.C. reined in her thoughts again. A vivid imagination had always plagued her as a child, but she'd never reacted in quite this physical a way to a man before. Just looking at him made her palms itch.

For the first time, she noticed the gun and her throat went dry. It was tucked into the waistband of his jeans, right above his exceptional-looking—

Stop it, she scolded herself. She could very well be looking at a killer. A ruthless, cold-blooded killer.

In that very instant, he whirled on her and she found herself looking down the barrel of a very big gun.

"Open the door slowly and keep your hands where I can see them. Don't make me shoot you."

3

"WHO IN THE HELL are you?" Nik asked as the tiny redhead stepped out of the cupboard.

"Who are you?" she countered.

"I'm a cop, so I get to ask the questions." She was such a little pip-squeak that he couldn't imagine that she'd played a part in the carnage in the church, but his thumbs had prickled again the moment he'd stepped back into the sacristy. And it didn't sit well with him that it had taken him so long to sense her presence in that cupboard.

"Who are you?" he demanded a second time.

"I'm the caterer. Now it's your turn."

Nik narrowed his eyes. For a little bit of a thing she had guts. Under other circumstances, he might have enjoyed it, but the church was getting crowded. The EMTs were dealing with Father Mike and Roman. He'd arranged for both of them to be transported to the new St. Jude's Trauma Center, and he'd sent the first crime-scene team to the choir loft because he'd wanted a few minutes alone with this body. He'd called his captain, and D.C. Parker would want a full report as soon as he disentangled himself from some big charity ball he was attending.

"What's your name?" he asked.

"You know, you don't look like a cop. Those clothes are a bit casual even for a dress-down Friday. Do policemen even have casual-dress days?" She lowered one of her hands and held it out to him, palm up. "Show me some ID."

Nik swept his gaze over her. "If you're not going to tell me your name, maybe I'll just call you Pipsqueak."

It gave him some satisfaction when she narrowed her eyes and her foot began to tap. She couldn't be more than five foot two, but her stance radiated enough attitude for a woman twice her size. She had her hair twisted up on her head, but a few red curls had escaped. Her ruffled front white shirt was tucked into black pants that showcased surprisingly long legs. His gaze lingered on them a moment before he shifted his attention back to her face. That was when he noticed the eyes. They were green and direct, and for a moment he saw nothing else.

"Well? How about it? You do carry ID, don't you?"

Annoyance and something else moved through Nik as he forced himself to blink and break eye contact. Then he gave her his cop smile, the one his partner Dinah said looked like a sneer. "Dream on, Pipsqueak. Let me make this as clear as possible. I not only ask the questions, I give the orders. Turn around, put your hands flat against the door of the cupboard, and spread your legs."

There was a beat before she did what he asked, and he couldn't prevent the ripple of admiration that moved through him. He'd always been a bit of a sucker for a woman with guts. Nik was halfway through patting her down when he realized that he'd made a huge mistake.

He had actually begun to enjoy the feel of those tight little muscles and soft curves beneath his palms. Dammit, he was a professional. This was a crime scene that needed his full attention.

The moment he straightened, she whirled to face him. In that second when their bodies brushed against each other, a blast of heat shot through him. What in hell—?

He took a quick step back, but he could tell by the way her green eyes darkened that she'd felt it, too.

"Who the hell are you?" he muttered, half to himself.

She lifted her chin. "I told you. I'm the caterer."

"Detective Angelis?"

Nik recognized the voice of the young officer he'd left with Father Mike, but he kept his gaze on the redhead.

"Now, you know *my* name. What's yours?"

"I'm J.C. Riley. I made the 911 call, and I want—"

He held up a hand to cut her off. "What is it, officer?"

"Sir, they're about to take the priest away."

Nik tucked his gun into the waistband of his jeans, then grasped the redhead around the waist, lifted and plunked her on the counter. "Stay put."

Following the officer out to the altar, he saw that the EMTs had loaded the priest onto a stretcher and that two officers were taping the area where the body had been. Another two crime-scene investigators stood on the altar steps. So much for his desire to quietly walk through the crime scene and think before his captain arrived.

Nik addressed his question to the medics. "How is he?"

"Unconscious, but stable. The bleeding has stopped."

That was good news. "And the man in the vestibule?"

"Still unconscious. They won't know how seriously he's injured until they run tests."

"I saw who shot Father Mike."

Nik whirled and nearly brushed right up against the redhead again. He scowled at her. "I told you to stay put."

She narrowed her eyes. "If you're a cop, shouldn't you be asking me some more questions? I certainly have some for you. Are the bride and the groom all right? I heard some shots from farther away—maybe from up in that choir loft. And what about Roman Oliver?"

Nik frowned. "What's your connection to Roman Oliver?"

Before he could stop her, she slipped past him and nearly made it to the gurney the priest was on. Grabbing her arm firmly, he said, "Look, lady—"

"Is Roman Oliver dead, too?"

Nik clamped down on his temper. "No. He'll be taken to the hospital. In the meantime, this is a crime scene, and since you think it's my *job* to ask questions, try answering the one I just asked. What is your connection to Roman Oliver?"

"None. But I thought I recognized him. His picture's been in the paper lately because of that big land deal. He came in the back way a short time after the groom arrived. At least, I assumed it was the groom. And someone used the name Roman while the fight was going on."

"Fight?" Nik asked.

"Yeah. It was a doozey. I didn't see it, but I could

hear it from the dining room in the rectory. That's where I was setting up the cake and the champagne. What about the bride and groom and the other woman, the blonde? Are they okay?"

Nik could feel his head beginning to spin. "The blonde?"

"She came in with the bride. She was carrying one of those big dress bags so I figured her for the maid of honor. I assumed the brunette was the bride because she was carrying the flowers and had a little crown of them on her head. Definitely bridal."

"You're sure that it was a blonde who came in with the bride?" The photo he'd seen of Sadie Oliver in the newspaper had been taken from a distance, but she'd had dark hair.

"I'm positive."

"How tall was she?"

"Short. About my height. Are they all right? I think some of the shots came from the choir loft. Have you checked up there?"

When she tried to step past him again, Nik tightened his grip on her arm.

"I saw the groom running along the choir loft right after the first shots. Is he all right?"

Frowning, Nik pulled her into the sacristy. When the two crime-scene officers followed, he said, "When you're finished with the body, see if you can find the bullets." He gestured toward the shattered mirror and the splintered doorjamb. Then he glanced around and spotted a door that opened off the sacristy. It was small and narrow, its only purpose being to provide access to a staircase he assumed led to one of the lofts that edged the sides of the church.

But it had exactly what he was looking for. Slipping his handcuffs out of his back pocket, he fastened one of the bracelets around the redhead's wrist and latched the other one around the pipe of the radiator in the stair-well.

"What do you think you're doing?"

"Looks like I've done it, Pipsqueak." So far, he hadn't expected one move she'd made so it was giving him more than a little satisfaction to have surprised her.

She whirled, quick as lightning, and poked a finger into his chest. "This is police brutality. I'm going to report you to your superior."

"You'll have an opportunity to do that." A hell of a lot sooner than he'd like, Nik thought. A quick glance at his watch told Nik that Captain D.C. Parker would be arriving soon, and he still wanted to walk through the scene.

"Better still, I'm going to scream."

Did she ever shut up? He met her eyes, and for an instant he felt that same odd sense of awareness he'd experienced before. This close, her eyes reminded him of a swiftly moving stream, the kind that warned of rapids ahead, the kind a man could easily get sucked into and drown.

Suddenly, he was aware of just how close she was. One more step and their bodies would be in full contact again. One more step and he could…

No. Nik slammed the brakes on the direction his thoughts were taking. What in hell was happening to him? He was a cop, and she was a material witness to a crime that involved his brother's best friend. That's what he should be concentrating on.

It took more effort than he liked to take a step back instead of forward, but once in motion, he moved all the way to the doorway. That way he could keep his eye on what the officers were doing in the next room. Then he took out his cell and settled the little debate he'd been having with himself since he'd recognized Roman Oliver. He was going to break a rule and give his brother Kit a call. He needed a second set of eyes, and Roman needed someone on his side—at least until they sorted everything out.

IT WASN'T UNTIL Detective Angelis reached the doorway that J.C. finally allowed herself to breathe. The sudden influx of air burned her lungs. In a second or two her brain cells would start working again. She hoped. She watched the detective punch a number into his cell. It really wasn't a good idea to look at him, but she couldn't seem to tear her gaze away.

"Hey, bro, this is Nik."

Time for a reality check, Jude Catherine. This was Detective Nik Angelis. He was investigating a case. A case she was involved in. And someone had tried to kill her. She had worrisome things to occupy her mind. Still, it was hard to forget the effect that the man seemed to have on her senses. A moment ago when he'd been standing so close to her, he'd very nearly kissed her. If he had—

Just the thought of that possibility had heat pooling in her center. J.C. reminded herself to take another breath. She'd never in her whole life reacted this…this…viscerally to a man. And he hadn't even kissed her. Yet.

She definitely had to get a grip. Nik Angelis was a stranger, and while he might be handsome, he was also annoying. He'd called her "Pips-queak," for heaven's sake! More importantly, there was a dead body not fifteen feet away in the next room. Father Mike and Roman Oliver were going to the hospital. And what about the others? Nik Angelis hadn't answered any of her questions about them. Were they dead? Then there was the man with the snake eyes…

And to top it all off, she was starving. If only she'd thought to stuff some of those almonds in her pockets. Then she remembered the candles…

J.C. took two quick steps before the handcuffs brought her up short.

Nik glanced at her as he pocketed his phone. "You're not going anywhere."

She lifted her chin. "I left candles burning in the dining room. Someone ought to check on them. And could you ask them to bring me back something to eat?"

"This isn't a restaurant and I'm not a waiter."

"If you were, you wouldn't make much in the way of tips with that attitude."

The smile he flashed was completely and unexpectedly charming. "You'd be surprised, Pipsqueak."

On second thought, she decided he'd probably make *great* tips. The man had the eye-candy thing going for him, plus a kind of animal magnetism. "Look, you'd better check on the candles if you don't want the whole place to burn down."

He moved to the door and signaled one of the officers. "Take someone with you and check out the rectory. There are some candles burning in the dining room."

"And bring me some almonds," J.C. called.

The officer glanced at Nik and he nodded. Then he leaned against the doorjamb and studied her for a moment. "Ms. Riley, let's start from the beginning. Tell me what you're doing here and what you saw."

"I'm here because I was catering the wedding reception."

That's your van in the parking lot? 'Have an Affair with J.C.?'"

"Yes. And you're Detective Nik Angelis."

"Of the San Francisco Police Department."

There was a beat of silence, and J.C. found herself thinking that here they were—not even really on a first-name basis—and they'd very nearly kissed.

"Do you have any idea where the bride and groom are?"

"They're not dead?"

"They're not even in the church. Neither is the blonde you mentioned."

"You've checked the choir loft?"

"Empty."

J.C. pressed a hand to her stomach as relief streamed through her. Had she been worried all along about the possibility of more dead bodies? Was the fear and adrenaline rushing through her body the reason she'd become so obsessed with Nik Angelis?

"Did you see anyone else enter the church?"

She shook her head. "No."

He pulled out a notebook. "When were you first contacted by the bride and groom?"

"I wasn't. I don't even know who they are."

Nik stared at her. "You catered the wedding and you don't know who the bride and groom are?"

"Father Mike was keeping it hush-hush. But he did drop the names, Juliana and Paulo. I thought they might be minor celebrities. Winners of *Survivor* or something like that."

"So you didn't know that they were Juliana Oliver and Paulo Carlucci?"

It was J.C.'s turn to stare as she let out a long low whistle.

"You do know them then?"

"Not personally. But I recognize the last names. Those two families are big business rivals, right?"

"Did the bride and groom arrive together?"

"No. I'd just brought the cake in when the two women arrived in a taxi. I told you before—I figured the young, dark-haired one for the bride, and the blonde for the maid of honor. Father Mike had told me to prepare cake and champagne for five—the bride and groom, the best man and maid of honor, and him." She frowned. "He didn't say anything about the body-guard."

"The bodyguard?"

"The dead man. He drove the groom here. You've got to admit he has the build. Of course, he might have been the best man."

"When did Roman Oliver arrive?"

"Maybe five minutes later. I didn't recognize him at first, not until the fight started and someone used his name."

"Tell me about the fight."

J.C. described the noises, and what she'd heard.

"When I heard the shots, I called 911 and ran across the walkway and into the sacristy. I nearly tripped over the big man's body. Then I heard Father Mike's voice from the altar and I got there just in time to see this man in a ski mask raise his gun."

"He was wearing a ski mask?"

"Yes."

"Then it wasn't Roman Oliver who shot Father Mike?"

"No."

Nik didn't allow himself to feel relieved. Not yet. Roman could have brought help if he'd come here to stop the wedding. "Did you see Roman at all after you entered the sacristy?"

"No. All I saw were the dead man, Father Mike and the man who shot him."

"So you're in the doorway, you see the guy with the ski mask pointing a gun at Father Mike. What happened next?"

"I yelled at him to stop and I threw my cell phone at him. I got him, too, but I was too late to save Father Mike."

"Maybe not. Father Mike took a bullet in the shoulder. I bet the shooter intended that bullet for his heart."

"Oh." J.C. let out a little sigh and felt her knees go suddenly weak. "Oooops," she said as she slid down the wall to the floor.

Nik got to her in two quick strides and squatted down, taking her hands in his. "You all right?" She didn't look all right. Her face had gone white. "You're not going to faint on me, are you?"

Her eyes sharpened then and her chin lifted. "I never

faint. I grew up with four brothers. There's not much I haven't seen. It's…just starting to sink in."

"Sir, I've got the almonds."

Nik gestured for them, and then handed the little silver bowl to J.C. When she'd finished a handful, he said, "So what happened after you hit the guy in the ski mask with your cell phone?"

"He whipped off the ski mask and pressed it against the back of his head. I must have hit him pretty hard. Then he turned and pointed his gun at me."

Nik noticed that her knuckles had turned white where she was gripping the silver bowl.

"His eyes were like a snake's. When I looked into them, I knew that he was going to kill me. So I ran and hid in the closet."

Guts, Nik thought. She had them in spades. And she'd used a cell phone to try to stop a killer. "Back to the blonde. Tell me about her. What did she look like?"

J.C. thought for a minute while she ate another almond. "I didn't see her face. She had her back to me the whole time she was walking into the church. But she's short and slender, and she's a girly-girl. Her suit was expensive and fashion-forward."

"You could tell all that from a back view?"

"Sure." She said it in the same tone that Sherlock Holmes might have used to say, "Elementary, my dear Watson."

"Do you know what happened next?"

J.C. shook her head. "Maybe Snake Eyes kidnapped them."

"Maybe." Nik didn't like that scenario, but he couldn't dismiss it. "I was close enough to get here within two or three minutes of your call to 911. Snake Eyes could have heard the siren and decided to bolt." At least he hoped that was the way it had gone down. If that were true, then there was a chance that the mystery woman and the bridal couple had taken off on their own steam. "Tell me about Snake Eyes again. Everything that you can remember."

She did, and when she got to the part where he was moving in on her and she was paralyzed, Nik gripped her hands again. He didn't like the fact that she'd raced into the sacristy after hearing the first shots. That had been foolhardy. And admirable. She'd saved the priest's life. Yet, she'd been scared to death. Hell, she was scared now just talking about it. He saw it in her eyes, felt it in the way she was squeezing his hands.

"I need more nuts," she said with a shaky voice.

Nik had a different idea. It was against all the rules, but the desire to kiss her had been building inside of him since she'd stepped out of that damn cupboard. He'd tried to ignore it, but he wasn't sure he wanted to anymore. He was the one in his family who'd had to struggle the hardest against a reckless streak. Kit was a dreamer and Theo was the intellectual, the politician. Becoming a cop had allowed him to channel his recklessness and his love of adventure and—he hoped—put it to good use. But he'd been thinking about kissing the redhead, and if he'd just get it out of his system then, maybe, his head would finally clear.

"Let's try this instead." He covered her mouth with his.

4

THE KISS WASN'T AT ALL what she'd been expecting. There were storms inside this man. She'd sensed them, seen them in his eyes, and she'd anticipated that his mouth would be hard, demanding, and that it would set off answering storms in her. Instead, he barely brushed his lips against hers.

J.C. moistened her lips with her tongue and tasted him. His flavor reminded her of something rich and forbidden. When she leaned closer for more, he released one of her hands and raised his to cup the back of her neck. Then he took his time, sampling, nipping, tracing the shape of her mouth with his tongue. A stream of thick, liquefying pleasure moved through her. His mouth was so soft, so warm. She could feel her blood heat, her muscles grow lax, her bones begin to melt.

When he drew away, she grabbed his shoulder with her free hand, absorbed the sensations of smooth, hot skin and hard muscle. "More."

"I'm with you there, Pipsqueak," Nik murmured as he leaned in again.

This time the kiss wasn't quite so gentle. And she didn't want it to be. His body was so lean and hard. And his hands—she could feel the pressure of each individual finger. But they weren't where she wanted them to be. Still the storm she'd expected, was beginning to crave, was building.

More. The sound of the word, the tone she'd used became a drumbeat in Nik's head. He'd intended to keep the kiss gentle, exploratory, but there was something inside of him that badly wanted to break free. When he nipped her bottom lip and heard her quick gasp, he very nearly released it.

On some level, he knew that he was losing his mind. Kissing a material witness to a murder when he should be walking the crime scene? He had to stop right now—but he didn't. Shifting onto his knees, he drew her up to hers and pulled her closer until her body was molded to his, soft and yielding. Heat flared. Her fingers dug into his shoulder, and he took the kiss deeper, devouring her.

Each little response—her throaty moan, the movement of her tongue on his—fueled the fire that was growing within him. She was so responsive, so generous. Her flavors weren't sweet. He'd been right about that. But he hadn't expected the endless variety that he was discovering as he probed one recess after another. Her mouth was every bit as eager and demanding as his.

Her body trembled, and in one quick move that shuddered through his system, she wiggled onto his lap until her thighs straddled his. He heard his heartbeat raging in his chest as he plunged deeper still.

More, more, more.

Need clawed through him. Anything he asked, she would give him. He could feel his control slipping and he at last found the strength to pull back.

They were both gasping for breath, both trembling. Nik wanted nothing more than to grab her again and finish what he'd started. Her eyes were dark, misted with pleasure. Pleasure that he'd given her, pleasure that he wanted—no, needed—to give her again.

"What—?" The word came out on a breath, and she shook her head as if to clear it.

His reckless streak threatened to break loose again. He could have her. He could shut the door all the way, turn the lock and take her. It would be wild and crazy and…absolutely impossible.

Dammit. He had a job to do, and she was interfering. He eased her back onto her knees. When he rose, he didn't like it at all that his own knees felt weak.

"Where are you going?"

Her voice was stronger now. He hoped that his would be, too. "It's been fun, Pipsqueak, but I have to do my job."

He walked out, pulling the door behind him and heard the thud of what he suspected was the little silver bowl as it made contact with the wood and plunked to the floor.

Nik almost grinned. Kissing J.C. Riley had been a mistake. Big-time. Instead of getting her out of his system, he'd embedded her in it—deep. He was going to have to figure out just what to do about that.

But first, he was going to do just what he'd said. His job. And number one on his list was bringing his captain up to date on what he knew or had surmised so far. He punched numbers into his phone as he strode back to the altar.

TWENTY MINUTES LATER, Nik and Kit were studying the taped outline where Roman Oliver's body had lain only a short time before. Nik had known when he'd called his brother that Kit would come immediately, and it had helped him to talk to Kit and to view the evidence through a second set of eyes. A glance at his brother's face told him that Kit was thinking the same thing that he was thinking.

There was no way around it. Roman was involved in what had gone on here. Sadie Oliver might be involved also. She hadn't come with either Roman or her sister Juliana—J.C. would have spotted her if she had. She'd probably come in through the front entrance. Now she and the bride and groom were all missing, and her purse had been left behind.

The best scenario Nik could come up with so far was that Roman had gotten wind of the wedding and had come to the church to talk his sister out of it. Then he'd gotten into a fight with Paulo Carlucci, and had shot the man in the sacristy, hopefully in self-defense. Then he'd followed Paulo up the stairs into the choir loft, where they'd struggled again and Roman had fallen or been pushed down the stairs.

He didn't have a theory about what part Sadie had played in all of this. But it wasn't going to look good to his captain that she'd left the scene of a crime. When he'd first gotten the call, the dispatcher had mentioned two 911 calls. He'd be able to find out if one had come from Sadie.

He shifted his gaze to the choir loft overhead. Of course, once one started theorizing about the blood on the walls of that little storeroom and the presence of J.C. Riley's Snake Eyes, the scenario got worse because it suggested that Kit's best friend and the man who'd once saved his sister's life had come here with murder in mind, and he'd brought some extra firepower with him.

Nik had a hunch that his captain was going to favor the latter scenario. Hell, he'd favor it himself if he didn't know Roman.

He studied the frown on Kit's face and knew that his brother's mind was traveling along the same path.

There was going to be pressure to close the case as quickly as possible. No one wanted any violence to erupt between the Oliver and Carlucci families. Sure, they'd been legit for half a century now, but Mediterranean blood ran hot. He ought to know, being Greek.

The press, once they got wind of it, was going to have a field day. The secret wedding of the children of two rival families, murder and mayhem—not to mention the disappearance of the bridal couple—was fodder for the kind of media circus that would keep the twenty-four-hour news channels going for days.

"Mind if I take a look at that room upstairs?" Kit asked.

Reining his thoughts in, Nik sent his brother a frown. "Of course I mind." But wasn't that why he'd called Kit in the first place—to fill his brother in on the evidence? He didn't want to believe that Roman Oliver was behind this any more than Kit did. More than that, he wanted to make sure that Roman had someone working on the case who was on his side. As a cop, he had to be objective, do his job. A P.I. had a lot more leeway. "When has that ever stopped you once you set your mind on something?"

"Never."

Still scowling, Nik handed Kit a pair of shoe covers. "The room's at the top of the stairs. Don't get in the way of my people, and don't touch a thing."

"Thanks, bro. I'll be careful."

Just then, the front door of the church blew open behind them, and a voice boomed, "There you are, Detective Angelis."

"Shit," Nik muttered under his breath. "It's the commissioner and my captain. Make it quick up there. There's a second staircase from the loft that leads down to the sacristy. Use it when you leave."

J.C. YANKED ON THE HANDCUFFS for about the tenth time. With each tug, she'd entertained the hope that she might be able to break free. Her Grandmother Riley had always told her to dream big. Evidently, getting out of police issue handcuffs was too big a dream.

Too bad Detective Angelis's brother Kit hadn't been carrying a spare key because *he* would have helped her. Although her conversation with him when he'd stumbled across her in the stairwell had been brief, she'd found Kit Angelis to be both kind and charming. She'd even accused him of being the "good cop" Nik had sent in to interrogate her. But unless she missed her guess, Kit Angelis had come to St. Peter's with an agenda of his own.

And except for the pretty face and those incredibly blue eyes, she wouldn't have guessed that the two men were even remotely related. When Nik Angelis had tapped the family gene pool, he'd passed on kindness and charm and loaded up on arrogance and rudeness instead.

Scowling at the radiator, J.C. vowed that she was going to make Detective Nik Angelis pay for his high-handed treatment of her. The little room he'd imprisoned her in was hot and stuffy. And he'd closed the door on her, so that the window air conditioner that had been fighting heroically to cool the sacristy couldn't even reach her. At least Kit had propped the door open when he'd left. But so far the cooler air hadn't made much progress into the room.

Worst of all, the handcuffs didn't even allow her to pace her anger off. There was no way that she was going to let Nik Angelis get away with this. Even if he *had* kissed her into a puddle of lust.

Okay, *that* could be the true cause of her anger with the hunky detective, J.C. silently admitted. Or perhaps it was because he'd stopped kissing her and sauntered off to do his job as if he did that kind of kissing every day and it didn't affect him in the least.

The problem was he'd simply destroyed her. Maybe had ruined her life. What if she never met another man who could make her feel that way?

Oh, God. She sat down on the radiator and dropped her head in her hands. The absolute worst of it was she wanted him to kiss her again. It didn't even seem to matter that on some level, she hated his guts.

The fact that she'd reacted to him the way she had simply didn't make sense. Unless it was due to an adrenaline rush. At the idea, her spirits perked up. Maybe that was it—because Nik Angelis was definitely not her type. He had a ton of qualities she didn't like in a man. He was pushy and impossible. Just like her father.

Oh, she loved her father dearly, but he was an Olympic contender when it came to manipulation and getting his own way. Patrick Riley was a big, gruff bear of a man whose hero in life was Joe Kennedy, and like J.F.K.'s dad, he wanted to found a dynasty. His second marriage to Alicia Hensen, heiress and socialite, had brought an aura of prestige and money to his political aspirations, and now he wanted his children married and bearing children. And her stepmother, oddly enough, was cut from the same cloth. They gave lie to the theory that opposites attract.

Her current plan as far as her parents were concerned, was to fly under both of their radar screens by devoting all of her energy to building up the reputation of her catering business. "Have an Affair With J.C." wasn't the talk of San Francisco yet, but it would be. In the meantime, it kept her too busy to date the sophisticated, eligible and incredibly boring males her stepmother was volleying at her like so many tennis balls.

Her two older brothers had fallen in and they'd already produced two grandchildren each. Her younger brothers, the twins, were finishing at Annapolis and had been granted a reprieve. That meant that Patrick and Alicia Harwood Riley were focused on her. She'd managed to slip out of their sights for a year by attending culinary school in New York. But now that she was back in San Francisco, her only excuse was her work. The weddings she was catering thanks to Father Mike were little plums that fate had dropped right into her lap, especially because they occurred on the weekends—prime date time.

The thought of Father Mike had her stomach

sinking, and once again she pictured those seconds that had seemed to happen in slow motion—the flash of fire and the deafening sound of the gun going off. She didn't even know how serious Father Mike's condition was. The least that Detective Nik Angelis could do would be to come back and fill her in.

Sensitivity was obviously another quality he'd missed when he'd dipped into the Angelis gene pool. She glanced down at her cuffs. He would have to come back to release her, and when he did, she would have a grip on herself.

Her adrenaline had settled. Reaching into her pocket, she took out a sugar-coated almond and popped it into her mouth. Once he'd released her from the handcuffs, she'd go her way and he'd go his.

J.C. frowned down at the handcuffs. Just as soon as she paid him back in spades.

"WHAT WE'VE GOT HERE is a time bomb," Commissioner Galvin said. "Do you think any of it has leaked yet, Angelis?"

"Hard to say, sir." Nik led the way up the aisle of the church. He'd already shown them the small room in the choir loft. "I've given orders to the officers, but the EMTs don't work for the SFPD."

"What's your take, Parker?"

Nik's boss, D.C. Parker, nodded in his direction. "I agree with Angelis. We've got two missing kids, a wounded priest and a dead man. And we've got Roman Oliver, the older brother of the bride-to-be who had plenty of motivation to put a stop to the wedding and who seems to be involved. We don't know what role the older sister played, but the fact that she left doesn't look good."

"She left her purse behind," Nik pointed out. "In my experience, a woman rarely does that. Maybe in her rush to help the bride and groom escape, she didn't have time to retrieve it."

"Nice theory, Detective," Parker said. "And in that case, we'll hear from her soon. Before the media gets hold of this and focuses on a more headline-grabbing explanation for her disappearance."

"The media will turn this whole thing into a circus," Galvin said. "We need to find the bride and groom fast."

"I agree." Nik had known that neither his captain nor the commissioner would be happy about the situation. D.C. Parker was a political player, but he was also a good cop. Commissioner Galvin, on the other hand, had his eye on advancement. The word was that he was using his position as a stepping stone to the mayor's office and perhaps one day the governor's job. "The priest said that someone wanted to kill the bride and groom."

"But Roman Oliver is in the hospital. Shouldn't they be safe?" Commissioner Galvin asked.

"We don't know that Roman is behind this," Nik noted.

"He's our prime suspect," Galvin pointed out.

"Perhaps, but there's a lot we don't know," Nik said. "Even if Roman is behind it, that puts him at risk if the Carlucci family decides to retaliate. I sent two men with him in the ambulance. We'll need to post men twenty-four-seven on both him and Father Mike."

"Right. Good thinking," Galvin said. "What about the other eyewitness—the caterer?"

"She'll need protection, too, of course. The man who shot Father Mike knows that she can ID him. He took off his ski mask when she hit him with her cell phone." Nik ushered the two men through the sacristy and into the small anteroom where he'd left J.C. She was seated on the radiator, and she shot him a look that nearly seared his skin.

Then her expression completely changed, and he watched in astonishment as she beamed a smile at the commissioner. "Uncle Chad? Is that you?"

"Jude Catherine? What are you doing here?" Commissioner Galvin moved forward and enveloped J.C. in a huge hug. When she tried to hug him back, her handcuffs clanged against the radiator pipe.

"What's all this?" Galvin frowned down at the handcuffs and then turned to Nik. "Why is my godchild in handcuffs?"

"Yes, Detective Angelis, I'm wondering that myself," Parker said.

"Mayor Riley is not going to be happy about this." Galvin shot a look at Parker and then at Nik. "I'm not going to enjoy explaining to him that a detective on my force handcuffed his only daughter."

Nik shoved his hands in his jeans pockets. Didn't that just figure? The little redhead was the commissioner's godchild and Mayor Riley's daughter. That certainly explained her habit of ordering people around.

Parker muttered under his breath, "An explanation, Angelis."

Before Nik could reply, J.C. answered, "He fastened

me to the radiator to keep me safe while he concentrated on the crime scene. He said he didn't want me mucking it up. He was only doing his job."

"Oh." Galvin turned his attention back to J.C. "But that still doesn't explain what you're doing here."

Nik simply stared at her. She'd just done her best to save his skin. He couldn't identify the emotions surging through him as he watched her straighten her shoulders and lift her chin.

"I'm the caterer. I've been running my own business for almost a year now, Uncle Chad."

"Your father has never mentioned it," Galvin said.

"No—"

"Wait," Galvin interrupted and turned to Nik. "Are you telling me this is the caterer who can identify the man who shot the priest?"

"The one and only," Nik said.

"She'll need protection," Galvin instructed Parker. "I want you to put your best man on her twenty-four-seven. That's what her father will demand when I talk to him."

"You're looking at my best man." Parker jerked his head toward Nik.

"Him?" Galvin and J.C. spoke in unison.

"The one and only," Parker replied.

Galvin looked Nik up and down. Then he slowly smiled. "Well, I guess if he managed to handcuff her to a radiator, he can handle her."

Nik met Parker's eyes. "Sir, this is my case. And you want me to babysit *her?*"

"You've got your assignment, Angelis. I'll handle the case personally. Your job is to stick to Ms. Riley like glue until we can wrap this up."

Shit, Nike thought as he looked at J.C. And if he read her expression right, she was thinking the same thing. This was not only the case of the century, it was one that involved someone close to his family—and he had to babysit the mayor's daughter.

5

DETECTIVE NIK ANGELIS was furious. J.C. sensed the anger radiating off him in waves and felt it in the hard grip of his fingers on her arm as he dragged her out of the church.

She dug in her heels as they circled her van. "I need to get my bag. I keep a change of clothes in it, and I'm assuming that you're not taking me back to my place."

He waited, saying nothing as she opened the doors and pulled a duffel out of the back of the van. He'd spent a fruitless five minutes trying to argue his way out of his new assignment. She could sympathize with his frustration because she hadn't been any more successful in her little debate with Uncle Chad. Their fates had been sealed when her uncle had called her father and convinced him that Detective Angelis was the only man for the job. Then her father had talked to Captain Parker, and that was that. Obviously, Nik Angelis blamed her for the fact that he was stuck with a babysitting job.

Babysitting. That's the term he'd used when he'd been talking to his captain. Just thinking about it had her own anger flaring up again. She sent him a scowl as he led her around to the other side of the van.

"What's going to happen to my van?" she asked as he jabbed his key into the door of a sporty little red convertible that didn't look at all like police issue.

"Parker will arrange to have it delivered to your place of business."

"What about the cake?"

"The cake? You're worried about the cake?"

"I *made* the cake," she objected. "I don't want it to go to waste. You can tell your captain to send it down to the precinct or whatever you call it. It's an exceptional cake. If cops like donuts, they'll—"

"Listen, Pipsqueak, let's get this straight. My job is to protect you, not take orders from you. This will go more smoothly if you remember I'm the boss."

He tightened his grip on her arm and planted his other hand at the small of her back, preparing to unceremoniously shove her into the front seat of his car as if she were a criminal. Slamming her hand down on the open door, she stood her ground. "Look, pal, I'm just as unhappy about this situation as you are."

"You think?"

The look he gave her dried her throat. Okay maybe she wasn't *quite* as unhappy as he was. But why was that? Then she recalled her visit from his brother. She'd thought at the time that it was a bit odd that a cop's family member was walking around the crime scene. J.C. moistened her lips. "This isn't just about babysitting me. This case has some personal meaning to you, doesn't it?"

Nik's eyes narrowed. "Maybe. Get in the car."

Once more she resisted the pressure of his hands. "Wait! We can figure a way around it. I have some suggestions. You might have noticed that my father has a real talent for bullying everyone who gets in his way."

"And your point is?"

"I have twenty-five years of experience wiggling around him. I'm sure we can work—"

Nik gripped her chin in his hand, leaned in close and clipped his words off like bullets. "Shut up and get in the car."

The moment he eased back to allow her to do so, she planted both hands on his chest and gave him one hard shove. The move caught him by surprise and he stumbled back a step, pulling her with him. That was when she felt a searing pain in her upper arm and heard a ping. Next thing she knew something that felt like a Mack truck had slammed her flat against the pavement.

It took a few seconds before the pain sang its way through her whole body, a few more for her senses to sort through the source of each separate ache. But finally, J.C. registered that her head hurt, her arm stung and Nik's weight on top of her had probably collapsed a lung. The tarmac was hot beneath her back, and Nik was swearing an equally hot blue streak in her ear.

For some odd reason the sound of his voice comforted her. He took time to draw in a breath, then lifted his head and said, "You all right?"

"I'm alive." She concentrated on that one small fact while Nik wiggled on top of her, drawing out both his gun and his cell phone. Flipping open the cell, he pressed one button and began to speak tersely into it.

J.C. took stock. She was definitely alive, but she was a little worried that she was becoming way too familiar with the sound of gunfire.

"Who shot at me?" she asked when Nik was through on his phone.

"My money's on your pal Snake Eyes."

That's where her money would have gone, too—to win, place and show. "That means he waited for me."

"We're on the same page there, Pipsqueak. And he wants you dead pretty bad to try for it with cops swarming all over the place."

She hadn't been scared before, not since Nik had arrived on the scene, perhaps because none of it had seemed real, but the thought of that horrible man hanging around, waiting for her to come out of the church, sent an icy arrow of fear through J.C.

Another thought occurred to her. "If you hadn't hand-cuffed me to that radiator, I would have run back to the rectory to blow out the candles. Then I probably would have started loading the cake and the champagne into my van. I'm like that. When I'm nervous, I like to keep busy." A tremor moved through her body. "He could have picked me off like a duck in a shooting gallery."

"It didn't happen." Nik met her eyes, his voice just as terse as it had been on his phone. "It's not going to happen. And you can take that to the bank. I've been assigned to protect you, and I'm good at my job."

She believed him. She thought she might believe anything he said when he was looking at her that way— as if he could see everything about her. And she was once again intensely aware of him, of the weight and warmth of his body on hers. This close, she could see the golden flecks in the darker brown of his eyes. J.C. watched, fascinated, as his eyes grew even darker and focused entirely on hers.

In the distance, she heard shouts, the sounds of running feet. In spite of that her awareness of Nik grew more and more intense. For the first time she realized that her legs were spread, and his were between them. She could feel the hard length of him growing even harder and pressing against her center. It wasn't just golden flecks she could see in his eyes. It was desire—as hot and as reckless as what was building inside of her.

Never taking his gaze from hers, he rocked into her once. J.C. felt as if she'd been caught in a backdraft of flames. It was a wonder that anything remained of her but cinders. He moved against her again, harder this time, and more heat shot through her. If he thrust against her once more, she was going to climax. Even now, she could feel the little ripples beginning. She had to stop them, but she wasn't at all sure that she could.

"You're so responsive," Nik murmured.

He knew, she realized. He knew that she was about to come.

"Is she all right?"

Nik jerked his head up, and in some part of her mind—whatever was left of it—J.C. recognized Captain Parker's voice.

"She's alive," Nik said. "Did you find the bastard yet?"

"I've got teams fanning out. They're checking the buildings in the area you said the bullet came from."

J.C. was finding it difficult to concentrate on what the two men were talking about. How could she when she was so aware of Nik? And she was so close to a climax. If either of them moved, she was very much afraid that she was going to come. She didn't even dare to breathe.

Instead, she concentrated on not wrapping her legs around him and finishing what he'd begun.

"Better keep her covered for a few more minutes," Parker said. J.C. caught the sound of footsteps retreating.

"Now," Nik whispered against her ear. Then he pushed against her and kept the pressure hard. "Come for me, now."

J.C. couldn't stop it, couldn't contain the huge wave of pleasure that was already pulsing through her. She sank into it, giving herself over to the orgasm and to the man who was giving it to her.

Somehow, she lost track of time, not sure how many seconds or minutes had passed before she finally latched on to a coherent thought. Opening her eyes, she found Nik regarding her steadily. She had the distinct feeling that her world was spinning out of control.

He levered himself up, then swore. "Shit. Your arm is bleeding. Why didn't you tell me that bastard shot you?"

She followed his gaze and saw that her shirt was torn, her upper arm red. "I might have if you hadn't distracted me."

But he wasn't listening. He was barking orders for an ambulance into his cell phone while he helped her into a sitting position, then ripped the tear in her shirt wider. Closing her eyes, she leaned her head back against the car. We have a problem, Houston, she told herself. More than one problem actually. First off there was Nik Angelis. This was a man who'd just given her the best climax of her life—and they hadn't even taken their clothes off. Never mind that he didn't even like her and that she'd just risen to the top of his jobs-he-most-hated list.

What in hell was she going to do about him?

Somehow it was easier to think about the problem of Snake Eyes, who seemed determined to kill her....

What in hell was she going to do about *him?*

NIK STOOD IN the doorway of the room they'd wheeled J.C. into and watched while a nurse inspected the wound in her arm.

"You're a lucky girl, Ms. Riley," the nurse said. "It's just a scratch."

That had been his own diagnosis; still, Nik felt the knot in his stomach ease just a bit when he heard the official words.

"My luck has just run out if you're thinking of sticking a needle in me," J.C. replied.

"Not my call," the nurse said with a chuckle. "I'm just supposed to clean it. The doctor makes the needle decisions."

"Does he accept bribes?" J.C. asked.

Nik nearly joined the nurse when she laughed. The fact that J.C. was back in fighting mode eased more of the tension that he'd been feeling. That had been a damn close call back at that parking lot.

Satisfied that she was in safe hands for the moment, he moved to the end of the corridor and signaled to the uniformed officer standing just inside the hospital entrance. Captain Parker had sent a patrol car to escort them to the emergency room as an added safety measure.

When the young officer reached him, Nik said, "I

have something I need to check on, so I want you to stand at Ms. Riley's door. No one but the doctor is to go in. And make sure he's the doctor, okay? Look at his ID tag."

"Yes, sir."

Nik was about to turn away when he added, "And under no circumstances are you to let Ms. Riley come out of that room until I get back. Handcuff her to a radiator if you have to. Understand?"

"Yes, sir."

Nik hurried into the nearest elevator and punched the sixth floor. That was where Roman Oliver was. He'd wheedled the information out of the nurse at the reception desk while J.C. was filling out forms. This wasn't his case—he was going as a friend, not as a cop, he tried to tell himself. And that was partially true. He'd already tried calling the desk, and no information about Roman's condition was being released. But he also wanted to see the players. And if Roman was conscious…

The elevator door slid open and as Nik stepped out, he could see the Oliver family through the glass wall of the waiting room. A quick scan told him that Sadie wasn't there and neither was Juliana. He'd had time to check and discover that the second 911 call had indeed been made by Sadie Oliver. It had been a long shot, but he'd been hoping to find her here.

He recognized most of the people in the room. Mario Oliver, Roman's father, looked every bit the successful multimillionaire businessman. He was tall and handsome with distinguished-looking gray hair. Right now he was talking to an attractive blonde who was seated on one of the couches, her hand on the arm of the young man sitting next to her. That had to be Mario's new wife, Deanna Mancuso Oliver, and her son Eddie.

Nik searched his memory. Mario had married Deanna…when? A year ago? Roman hadn't been totally pleased about the marriage, and Kit had accepted an invitation to the wedding to lend moral support. The only other people in the waiting room were a uniformed officer sitting in a chair near the door and a tall man in his early thirties standing near a TV set. That had to be Michael Dano, who headed up the legal department. If Nik remembered correctly, Sadie Oliver worked under him at Oliver Enterprises.

Nik noted that the TV was tuned to Channel Five News. Carla Mitchell, TV Five's star correspondent, was standing on the steps at St. Peter's Church, and the flash headline beneath her read Murder and Mayhem at a Wedding.

How long would it be before the press would be camped out in front of St. Jude's, he wondered. When he spotted a uniformed officer standing sentinel in front of one of the doors, he headed toward him.

"How is he?" Nik asked as he showed the officer his ID.

"I don't know, sir," the officer replied. "They've got him hooked up to a lot of machines."

Nik nodded as he pushed the door open.

"The doctors don't want anyone going in, sir. They asked me to—"

"I won't go in," Nik said. He didn't have to. Roman's head was wrapped in bandages and his face was pale. The only sounds in the room were the beeps and hums of the various machines. As Nik listened to them and watched the man who was attached to them, images flashed through his mind—Roman swimming to shore with Philly holding on to his back, Roman playing tennis with Theo and beating him, Kit arm wrestling with Roman at The Poseidon. Roman joining the entire Angelis clan on the dance floor.

"You just missed your brother, Detective."

Nik turned to see Mario Oliver approaching. "I'm sorry about this, sir. How is he?"

"Are you here in an official capacity?"

Nik hesitated for a moment. "Maybe you could call it semiofficial. I'm not assigned to this case. I arrived first on the scene at St. Peter's and called it in—Kit must have told you that already. But I do want to find out what happened tonight. Have you heard from your daughter Juliana yet?"

Mario studied him for a moment, then seemed to reach a decision. "No, I haven't heard from her."

"And your daughter Sadie?"

Something flickered in Mario's eyes. "We haven't been able to reach her yet."

Nik glanced back into the room where Roman was lying. "How is he?"

"The doctors say he has a skull fracture. They're more worried about the swelling at the base of his spine. If it doesn't go down by morning, they're going to have to operate. Until they reach that decision, they're keeping him sedated. They don't want him to move. I've already given that information to your captain."

"Do they think he'll recover?"

"If you're asking if he'll be paralyzed, they don't know yet. But they're hopeful."

Keeping his eyes on Roman, Nik asked, "Kit filled you in?"

"Yes."

Nik met Mario's eyes again. "I'm going to do everything in my power to find out what really happened at that church."

Mario nodded. "Your brother said as much a short while ago. And I'll be doing the same. I'm not afraid of the truth, Detective. My Roman didn't do what he's being suspected of."

"Did you know about the wedding, Mr. Oliver?"

"Mario? Is there a problem?"

Nik turned to see Michael Dano approaching.

"No," Mario said. Nik wasn't sure whose question the older man was answering.

Mario made the introductions, then said to Dano, "Detective Angelis is Kit's brother. He's going to help us find the truth."

As Nik took his leave, he was pretty sure that Michael Dano wasn't as convinced of that as Roman's father was.

6

"WHERE ARE WE GOING?" J.C. asked as Nik pulled his car out of the emergency room parking lot. It was the first time she'd spoken to him since they'd arrived at the hospital.

"Somewhere you'll be safe," he replied.

"A safe house?"

"Technically, it's not a safe house. But you'll be safe. It's where I live."

Silence fell in the car. Nik sensed that it wasn't an easy silence for either of them. They hadn't talked yet about what had happened right after she'd been shot and they'd been lying on the pavement. He'd given it more than a little thought during the ride to the hospital and then after he'd visited Roman while waiting outside her room. So had she, he wagered. His own conclusions did not make him happy. The attraction he felt for J.C. Riley was so strong, so primitive, that his control around her seemed to be touch and go. Mostly go.

He couldn't allow that to continue. If he was going to do his job and protect her, he had to keep his relationship with her strictly business.

J.C. turned in her seat to look out the rear window. "How do you know we're not being followed?"

A valid question, he thought. He'd dismissed his police escort because he thought it unlikely that anyone had tailed them to the hospital. "There's a good chance that the shooter took off as soon as he took that shot. Parker checked the neighborhood pretty thoroughly. And I took some precautions on my way to the emergency room. If he's smart, he'll check the emergency rooms, and eventually he'll learn you've been there. But it's doubtful that he could get that information this quickly."

"You're sure of that?" She glanced through the rear window again, and Nik noticed that her hands were clasped tightly together in her lap, the knuckles white. She'd been a real trooper in the E.R., but reaction was setting in.

"Just to be sure, let's try this." At the next corner, he took a quick left turn the wrong way onto a one-way street.

"What are you—"

"Tell me if you see anyone following us."

She glanced back. "No."

At the end of the street, he took another left, then a right at the following corner. J.C. kept her eyes glued to the rear window. After a few more minutes of the zigzag pattern, he asked, "Why catering?"

"What?" She shifted her gaze to him.

"Why catering? It seems an odd career choice for a rich girl."

Her eyes narrowed. "Really? I suppose you think rich girls spend their time shopping, having manicures and flying to Paris for lunch?"

Nik shrugged. "Toss in a little charity work, and that about sums it up." One glance confirmed what he'd heard in her tone. She was annoyed—but her knuckles were no longer white.

"Actually, I'm curious." He met her eyes for a moment. "Really. We've got a half-hour drive ahead of us." That was a lie, but talking would take her mind off the shooting. "Why catering?"

"I'll tell you if you put the top down. It's a crime to have a car like this and drive it with the top up. I may have to make a citizen's arrest."

He'd put it up after the shooting at the church, but since they weren't being followed, he released the lever, and with a push of a button, the ragtop hummed back. He sent her a look. "Now, why catering?"

"I got into it by chance. I received a liberal arts degree from Stanford, which prepared me for nothing and everything. But I love movies so I applied to NYU with some idea of doing some grad work in film."

"What films are your favorites?"

"I like the classics—Hitchcock, Billy Wilder."

"*It Happened One Night* was a great film."

"What's your favorite?" she asked.

"A more modern classic. *Raiders of the Lost Ark* has never lost its charm for me. *High Noon*'s my runner-up."

"I'm attached to *E.T.*, perhaps because it was the first movie I ever saw, and I love Redford and Newman in *The Sting*."

"Good flicks, but I distracted you. You were telling me how you got into catering."

She smiled. "As I said, by chance. I was in New York for an interview at NYU, and they took me to the American Culinary Institute for lunch. It's a restaurant where chefs in training prepare the menu for that day, and that was it. I knew that I wanted to go there. What made you decide to become a cop?"

"I suppose you could say it was fate, too. One day I got picked up for shoplifting. I was fourteen, and there was this group of boys at school that I admired. They were a little older and they had all the girls and a kind of prestige. I guess I wanted to fit in. My cousin Dino warned me they were trouble, but I knew better. I always knew better in those days."

J.C. raised an eyebrow. "In those days?"

He shot her a grin. "Okay. I always know better. One day after school, these guys invited me to come along, and before I knew what they were up to, we were in this store, and I was told I had to steal something. It was a sort of initiation ritual. I did it, and I got caught by a cop in plain clothes. I must have looked scared as hell because he didn't charge me. It helped that I hadn't left the store." Nik rolled his eyes. "Clearly, I wasn't going to become the next super thief."

"What happened?"

"The cop cut me a break. I begged him not to tell my father, and he agreed, providing I came down to the precinct every day after school for a full month. My job was to view firsthand the kinds of felons who were arrested and booked on a daily basis. It was supposed to scare the shit out of me and it did. But it also made me want to become a cop. There's a daily challenge to the job that really appeals to me."

"You like seeing if you can meet it," she said.

Surprised, Nik turned to her and saw understanding in her eyes. He nodded. "There's that. And there's also the fact that John Kelly made a difference with me. I liked the idea of being able to do the same for someone else someday."

They drove on in silence for a while, and Nik had time to reflect on the fact that about fifteen minutes had passed and they'd neither argued nor ordered each other around. Perhaps they'd reached a new plateau.

The illusion crumbled the moment they turned into his aunt Cass's driveway and the house came into view.

"Good grief." She turned to face him. "It's got a turreted tower and gardens and a view of the Pacific. Plus there's a huge pond over there. What kind of a cop are you, Angelis, that you can afford a place like this?"

He stopped the car and turned to meet her eyes. The bad news was she was back in insult mode. The worse news was that he was beginning to like her that way. There *was* a part of him that badly wanted to clip her right on the chin. But there was another part of him that realized her mouth and her bravado was the way she was coping with what had happened to her. That part of him, the part that was beginning to understand her, wanted to simply take her in his arms and hold her. But if he did, there was a good chance that they would finish what they'd started in that parking lot. He couldn't seem to be near her and not want to touch her. To have her.

Telling himself that he wouldn't follow through on his desire was a lie. The best he could hope for was that he could delay the timing until she was safe. In the meantime, he prayed for both patience and control.

"Relax, Pipsqueak. I'm the kind of a cop who has an aunt who owns a place like this. She inherited the place from my grandfather."

J.C. turned back to study the house. "No shit? My stepmother would kill to own this place. All she'd need is one look, and she'd have a Realtor knocking down your front door with an offer you wouldn't be able to refuse."

The admiration in her voice had any annoyance he was still feeling fading away. Truth be told, he loved the house. "My great-grandfather built the place with the money he made building boats. My brothers and sister and I were raised here after our mother died. Ironically, it was a freak boating accident that took both my mom and my uncle Demetrius, my aunt Cass's husband."

She reached out to cover his hand. "I'm sorry."

"It was a long time ago. After that, we all moved in here with Aunt Cass and her son, Dino. A couple years ago, we all chipped in and renovated the place into individual apartments. Now my dad lives over in the gardener's cottage, my brothers and I have apartments on the second and third stories, and my sister Philly and Aunt Cass have individual apartments on the first floor. And Aunt Cass has an office where she runs her psychic consulting office."

"Your aunt is a psychic?"

"Yes." He went perfectly still for a moment. He usually didn't just blurt that information out to people he'd only just met. Some people had a very low opinion of psychics.

"That's so cool. Have you inherited some of her abilities? I read that those kinds of talents are supposed to run in families."

Since admiration and curiosity was all he could read in her eyes, he said, "My sister has a talent with animals. Aunt Cass says she can talk to them."

"She's a Dr. Dolittle?" J.C. asked.

"I suppose that's one way to describe it."

"Amazing. I can't wait to meet her and your aunt, too. What about you? What's your…specialty?"

"I'm a cop. A good one. That's all."

"I bet it's not. Tell me. C'mon. Your secret will be safe with me."

The woman just never gave up. Exasperated, Nik said, "I wouldn't call it psychic, but my thumbs start to prick whenever there's danger or a disaster threatening."

"'By the pricking of my thumbs, something wicked this way comes.'"

Damn. She even knew the rhyme. "Something like that," he said. "Nothing that's going to get me on *Oprah*. You were saying that your stepmother would kill for this place."

Her eyebrows lifted. "Changing the subject, Detective?"

"Yeah."

Nodding at him, she glanced around. "My stepmother Alicia would take one look at this porch, the gardens and that lovely pond and she'd start planning a dozen different parties for my father's reelection campaign. Lunches, brunches, cocktail soirees. Her specialty is garden parties—the kind you have to wear a hat to."

"Do you cater them?"

She shook her head. "Not yet. Alicia and my dad are still sort of adjusting to my career choice. They'd prefer that I marry, settle down and produce children. If I appeared at one of their parties as the caterer, that might send the wrong signal to the string of eligible bachelors that Alicia is always introducing me to. Most of them seem to be looking for a Stepford wife."

"That's not you."

"You got that right."

Nik pulled to a stop in front of the house, got out of the car and circled it to open her door. He wasn't comfortable with what he felt when he imagined a string of eligible men parading past J.C. Not jealousy, certainly. And not fear. That was ridiculous.

"You have something against marriage?" He kept his hand on the small of her back as he guided her up the stairs.

"No. I merely have something against marriage right now. I need to be focused on growing my business. And if I do eventually marry, it won't be to provide my father with the dynasty he's determined to create. Or to provide my husband with the same thing. Not that I'm particularly worried about that right now. Luckily, I'm not exactly the tall, blond, trophy wife type that the men on my parents' list are looking for, if you know what I mean."

Nik was uncomfortably aware that he did. Her trophy wife description was too close a match to Dinah's description of the women he dated. Not that he intended to marry any of them.

"What about you? What are your feelings about marriage?"

"I haven't given it much thought. What will it take to convince you to marry?" Now where had that question come from, Nik wondered. It had just seemed to pop out.

"I think that I'll only get married to a man that I simply can't live without. You know—the man that the Fates intend me for, if you believe in that kind of stuff."

Nik's thumbs began to prick.

"I'm not sure that I do, so I figure that I'll probably end up being single. How about you?"

"Me?" Nik opened the door and ushered her into the foyer and toward the oak staircase that circled upward.

"This is lovely." She nearly crooned the words as she ran her hand along the gleaming banister. "And that chandelier—it's out of a fairy tale."

"My apartment is on the third floor," he said, guiding her up the stairs.

They climbed the three flights in silence, and he was just breathing a sigh of relief that the conversation had veered off from marriage when she asked, "Do you believe that there's a woman in the world who's just meant for you?"

For a moment, he didn't say a thing. He merely gazed at her as she stood there on the stairs in the house his great-grandfather had built, and he realized that she somehow looked right there.

No, thought Nik. No way. No how. The idea was an aberration. He and J.C. Riley might have a primitive attraction to one another. That was one thing. And they might have a few things in common. But in spite of those facts, they were as different as night and day.

7

NIK USHERED J.C. into his apartment, shut the door, then stood rooted to the spot as she moved around. She turned on a floor lamp, then picked up his TV remote and returned it to the wicker basket where he kept the other remotes.

He'd never brought another woman to his home. Perhaps that's why he felt a bit...odd as she roamed. Was it just nerves that had him hesitating on the threshold? He tried to see the place as she was seeing it. It certainly wasn't neat. He'd stripped out of his T-shirt after his morning run along Baker Beach and left it over the back of a chair. And his running shoes were on the floor nearby. An empty coffee mug and plate remained where he'd dumped them on the coffee table. She probably thought he was a slob.

He'd picked the leather couches for comfort rather than style. They were tan, rather plain he supposed. And there wasn't a lot of furniture. No paintings on the wall, and he'd chosen blinds instead of drapes. The only color in the room was offered by the Oriental rug, with its tones of deep blue, rust, ivory and dark brown.

Philly had once called his décor "spare as a monk's quarters," and he supposed she was right. J.C. had turned her attention to his bookshelves, running her fingers along some of the spines. She picked up a framed photo, studied it for a moment, then turned to him. "You're a sailor. This looks like quite a storm."

He knew the picture she was looking at. He'd been twenty, a bit on the reckless side, and he was on his sailboat, *Athena*. A storm had come up suddenly, and he'd nearly lost the battle getting the boat in. His fingers had started pricking before the wind had picked up, but he'd ignored the premonition. His struggle with the sea had been touch and go for a while, and he could still recall the thrill of victory he'd felt when he'd finally gotten the boat onto shore.

Then he'd had to face his family. He knew when he'd seen the look in his father's and aunt's eyes that he'd been careless and selfish. It had been a similar storm that had taken his mother's and his uncle Demetrius's lives. But he'd kept the photo that Theo had snapped to remind himself of that day—of the exhilaration he'd felt, as well as his responsibility to his family.

"You must be a very good sailor," J.C. said as she set the photograph back on the shelf.

Nik shrugged. "I'm Greek." And lucky, he thought.

With a nod, she picked up a leather-bound volume. "Greek myths. I've never sailed, but I read all of these when I took this mythology course. Of course, I read the Roman and Celtic ones, too. You'll think this is silly." She glanced at him, then looked away. "The first time I saw you, I thought of Adonis."

"Really." Adonis, the lover, he thought, a man with the almost impossible task of handling two women. Personally he didn't envy the guy. He was having enough trouble trying to figure out how to handle just this one. It occurred to him then that handling a woman had never posed much of a challenge before he'd met J.C.

Setting the volume back carefully on the shelf, she picked up the newspaper he'd read that morning and left in a rumpled heap on the couch, then the empty coffee mug and plate, and carried them through the archway that led to his small kitchen. "I'm starving," she said. "Do you mind if I whip something up?"

Following her, he watched as she put the newspaper in the recycle bin, placed the dishes in the sink, then ran hot water to rinse the plate. She was tidying up. And it was a shock to realize that he was enjoying having her here, puttering around in his home.

She opened his refrigerator, then glanced over her shoulder. "There's no food. Don't you eat?"

It was an accusation. She was definitely back in J.C. mode again. "Don't you stop eating?"

Her chin shot up. "I didn't have dinner. I was shot, I lost some blood, and at the hospital, they didn't offer me anything. When I give blood, they at least serve cookies."

"I've got beer and bottled water and…"

She sent him a withering look. "Moldy cheese and a bag of salad greens that's long past its expiration date." Scooping it up with two fingers and holding a hand under it in case it leaked, J.C. carried it to the garbage can. Then she closed the refrigerator door with a little snap and began to methodically search his cupboards. By the time she'd made her way down the wall that was lined with cabinets, she'd pulled out an empty cereal box, two empty boxes of crackers and a bag of stale potato chips.

"I'm starving, and your cupboards make Mother Hubbard's look plentiful. Do you at least have a stash of chocolate somewhere?"

Nik shook his head, studying her. "You eat when you're nervous or frightened. Which are you?"

She lifted her chin. "I'm hungry. It's nearly eleven and I haven't had anything to eat for dinner but those sugar-coated almonds."

"I think you're nervous because we're alone here in my apartment."

"You don't make me nervous, Detective."

"Oh, I think I do." Most of his own tension eased. "Maybe we should talk about what happened between us in the parking lot. Clear the air and lay some ground rules."

He waited a beat and when she didn't reply, he said, "I've been thinking it over, and I'd like to start by saying that it was a mistake."

She flinched. Not physically, but he saw it in her eyes and cursed himself. Taking a step forward, Nik continued, "Let me explain. You're in mortal danger, and my job is to make sure you're not killed. When I kissed you, I didn't know that Parker would assign me to be your bodyguard. But even then, I shouldn't have been making a move on a material witness. And what we did—what I did—in the parking lot…that was inexcusable."

J.C. held up a hand. "Stop right there. I get it. It's not politically correct to…fool around with your…your… You're going to have to help me out here. What am I?"

"I'm trying to figure that out."

"Cute. I'm talking about the correct term. You're the bodyguard and I'm the what?"

"Assignment."

"Okay." She tucked some loose curls behind her ear. "Well, I've been thinking, too."

He moved to the refrigerator and he wasn't displeased when she scooted out of his way. "Water," he said. He extracted a bottle, offered to her. When she refused, he opened it and drained half. It did nothing to quench the heat that was building inside of him.

"You are attracted to me, right?"

Nik nearly dropped the water bottle. Was he ever going to predict what she would say or do next? "Yeah. I think we've established that."

"And I'm attracted to you. I don't usually...I mean, I've never...what happened in the parking lot...I...I never..." She let out a little huff of breath. "That was a first for me."

He took two steps toward her before he stopped himself. She'd moved to the other side of the small island in the center of the room. It took every ounce of strength he had not to follow her. "It was a first for me, too, but..."

"Could you *just* let me finish?"

She'd fisted her hands on her hips and impatience radiated from her in waves. It occurred to Nik that he was dealing with two different women here—the vulnerable one who had to eat to chase off nerves and the fiery one who dished out killer looks and ordered people around like a drill sergeant. Was that why she fascinated him so? He couldn't help but wonder which one he would find when he took her to bed. Then he firmly pushed the thought away. "Go ahead."

"I had some time to think while that nurse was giving

me a tetanus shot. I hate needles so I had to distract myself some way. We agree that we have a problem. We're
attracted to one another, but hanky-panky between a
bodyguard and his assignment is not on a good cop's
to-do list. Right?"

"I'm with you so far."

"Now, I can only speak for myself about this part.
But whenever you're close to me, I lose brain cells—
and I don't seem to have any control whatsoever. Each
time you touch me, I want you."

He wasn't happy about the fact that she could have
been speaking for him, too.

"I thought at first that it was related to the danger I was
in—a sort of side effect of the adrenaline rush, you
know?"

Nik nodded.

"But I'm not in any danger right now, and I still
want you."

The woman had a mouth that was going to get them
both in trouble, he thought.

"And then we've got this other thing—the fact that
someone is trying to kill me."

"I'm with you there, too, Pipsqueak."

"Well." J.C. drew in a deep breath and let it out. "I
came up with a kind of solution while I was trying to
ignore that needle at the hospital. I figure if we have to
put a lot of effort into not kissing again and keeping our
hands off of each other, that's going to distract us from
figuring out a way to get Snake Eyes. So I think we
ought to give in to our mutual attraction and get it out
of our system."

Nik should have raised a hand, or said something.

But the hell of it was he could hear his own brain cells clicking off.

"What I propose is that we use each other, the way sex buddies do."

He blinked and said hoarsely, "Explain sex buddies."

"A sex buddy is someone you call on when all you want is really hot sex. No strings. No romance. No emotional involvement. And no work. Relationships are always such a lot of work, while sex buddies are very low maintenance. I think it fits our situation to a *T*."

Something twisted hard in Nik's gut as he circled the counter toward her. "You have sex buddies? Who? How many?"

"No. I don't have any." She backed away three steps. "Yet. I read about it in *Cosmo* and I maybe was thinking about it, but I've been too busy. Anyway, right now I'm talking about you. And me."

She backed up another three steps, and he followed, but she didn't stop talking.

"I think this sex buddy thing is perfect for us. We're going to have to work together to stop Snake Eyes, and we have this kind of primitive attraction for one another, and…"

It gave him a great deal of satisfaction to see her eyes grow huge when he used his hands to cage her against the wall.

"And…" he prompted.

She moistened her lips. "It just seems like the logical solution."

The one thing it wasn't was logical. There wasn't anything in the least bit rational in the way he felt about her. Or about her solution to their problem.

"How about it?" she asked.

Nik tried to think about it. The problem was, his brain had lost a lot of blood. Hell, he thought, if J.C. Riley was in the market for a sex buddy, he'd fill the bill. "Okay."

"Okay?" He was close again, and J.C. could feel her brain cells clicking off like so many little electric lightbulbs.

He rubbed a thumb over her bottom lip. "Has the cat finally got your tongue, Pipsqueak?"

"Did I…convince you that it…won't be a mistake?" His mouth was only an inch from hers, and any brain cells that hadn't shut down had dimmed.

"No." Nik angled his head and nibbled his way along her jaw. He was barely touching her, but she could feel it right down to her toes. "This is definitely a mistake. A big one. So we'll have to make it count, won't we?"

"Mmm-hmmm." Every single part of her—blood, bone, muscle, sinew—went suddenly into meltdown. She wanted to wrap her arms and legs around him just as much as she had in the parking lot, but she didn't have the strength. If her back hadn't been against the wall, if he hadn't been standing right there in front of her, she would have been in a puddle at his feet.

"I…need…" Her breath caught in her throat when he captured her earlobe between his teeth.

"What do you need, Pipsqueak?"

Think. "A name for you."

He lifted his head and looked at her. "It's Nik."

She shook her head. "No, I mean a nickname. I think…Slick."

He frowned. "Why would you call me that?"

"Why do you call me 'Pipsqueak'?"

"Because you're a tiny little bit of a thing, and you never stop talking." And then, as if he'd clearly explained everything, he began to use his mouth and his tongue and his teeth on her neck.

J.C. pressed her hands flat against the wall behind her for support as wave after wave of pleasure rushed through her. He wasn't touching her anywhere else. He was just using that incredible mouth of his on her neck, but she felt as if he were touching her everywhere. She certainly wanted him to.

Suddenly he stopped. "Open your eyes."

She did. "Did you change your mind?"

"No. I want you to undress for me."

She was willing strength into her arms when he eased away from her. The distance helped. She managed to unknot her tie and pull it off. "You like watching a woman strip?"

"Always. But I thought I'd try to slow things down for both of us. You came fast when we were in the parking lot." He met her eyes. "And the next time I do you, I want your clothes off."

The next time he did her? Just hearing him say the words had her inner muscles clenching. The man could probably make her come just by talking to her. And she could see in his eyes that he knew it. No wonder. Hadn't she just spent some time telling him what kind of sexual power he had over her?

Moving a step toward him, she looped her tie around his neck. Maybe it was about time that she figured out what she could *do* to *him*. Keeping her eyes on his, she unfastened her cuffs and pulled her shirt out of the waistband of her pants. Then starting at her throat, she slipped the buttons free one by one. Nik's gaze tracked her progress—and he was exciting to watch. When she'd finished, she waited a beat, then opened her shirt, shrugged her shoulders and let it slip to the floor.

His eyes were riveted on her bra. "What an unexpected surprise."

J.C. felt heat rise to her cheeks. She had a weakness for pretty and expensive lingerie. The bra she was wearing was cream-colored lace and silk, and as he continued to look at it, she could feel her nipples harden. A hot little thrill rippled through her when she saw that his jaw had hardened and he'd clenched his hands into fists.

Slowly, she moved her hands to the waistband of her slacks.

"Let me." His voice was rough and he moved fast, pushing her hands aside.

"What happened to slowing things—" She broke off when he pulled down her zipper and snaked one hand beneath her panties to cup her.

"Change of plan. This is what I wanted to do when we were lying on the pavement." He slid a finger between her folds and then into her.

Her muscles clenched around him. "Stop." But her body was already arching toward him, moving of its own accord. And her breaths were coming in gasps. "I'm going to come again. I can't help myself."

"You don't have to." His other arm went around her to support her. "Isn't this what a sex buddy is for?"

The orgasm shot through her in a widening wave that spread and spread—until it finally tossed her over an airless peak.

AFTERWARD NIK HELD HER on his lap, his cheek pressed against hers. His fingers were still inside of her and he could feel the last ripples of her climax pulsing against them. He couldn't seem to pull them out. They were exactly where he wanted to be. Where he needed to be. He'd been wrong when he'd thought she was two women. In addition to the vulnerable woman and the drill sergeant, there was also the passionate woman who exploded whenever he touched her.

No woman had responded to him so strongly before—and they had yet to progress beyond foreplay. He couldn't help but wonder how far they could still take each other.

When he began to move his fingers again, she placed her hand on his and stilled them. "This can't be all one-sided. I'm *your* sex buddy, too."

The moment he removed his hands, she wiggled off of his lap. "What do you want me to do to you, Slick?"

Slick. It was a ridiculous name—except when she said it.

Kneeling in front of him, J.C. pulled his tank top free of his jeans. "I think it's your turn to strip."

"You like to watch men strip?" he asked.

When she met his eyes, he saw a glint of mischief in hers, and it delighted him.

"There's no time like the present to find out."

"Agreed." He gripped the edge of his tank top and pulled it over his head.

She scooched a few more feet away. "Stand up."

Nik bit back a smile as he did what she ordered. His little drill sergeant had returned. "You're a constant source of surprise, Pipsqueak." He'd never stripped for a woman before. Well, yes, he had—but not intentionally, not as a show. Watching her as he unzipped his jeans, he decided that as foreplay, stripping had definite potential.

He stepped out of his jeans. Her gaze riveted on his black briefs.

"Very sexy," she said.

He hadn't thought he could get any harder, but he'd evidently been wrong. Slipping his thumbs beneath the elastic, he lowered them slowly.

"Wow!" She licked her lips.

"You're not going to get all nervous on me and demand that I feed you…."

She met his eyes and he saw the glint of mischief again. "Maybe." J.C. moved forward then on her knees and took him very carefully into her hands.

He barely suppressed a moan when he felt those slender, delicate fingers close around him.

"But perhaps I've found the perfect snack."

The moan escaped as her mouth closed around him, soft, hot. The quick flick of her tongue had his knees going weak. And when she continued to use her tongue on him, he felt his control stretch as thin and tight as a high wire. Before it could snap, he grasped her head in his hands and eased her away.

"That's not fair," she complained as he shifted his hands to her shoulders and drew her to her feet. "Turnabout's fair play. I wanted to make you come."

"You're going to." Then to prevent himself from taking her right there on the kitchen floor, Nik lifted her, tossed her over his shoulder and strode toward his bedroom.

"This isn't very romantic," she complained.

"Sex buddies don't need romance," he reminded her as he dumped her on the bed.

He'd expected a flare of temper. Perhaps, that's what he'd wanted. But she surprised and delighted him again by laughing. There she was—spread-eagled on his bed laughing. Her hair had loosened and it looked like bright red flames against the white comforter.

And he wanted her mindlessly. Moving quickly, he took a condom from the drawer in his nightstand.

She stopped laughing then and levered herself up on her elbows. "I want to put that on you."

"Next time. If I get any more help from you, I won't last long enough to get inside of you." She was still wearing her bra and panties, but he couldn't wait another minute. Joining her on the bed, he spread her legs and made space for himself between them. Then moving aside the thin barrier of lace, he entered her in one hard stroke. She was so hot, so wet, and tighter than he could have imagined. He tried to withdraw and couldn't, not with her muscles gripping him and pulling him even deeper.

"Look at me, J.C., and say my name."

"Nik."

He managed to move, a small rocking stroke.

"I'm coming again. I can't stop it."

"Don't try." He drew out and thrust in harder, deeper, until she completely sheathed him. The first hot ripples of her climax enclosed him, pulling at him, and as he watched her eyes darken and mist with pleasure, the first ripple of his own release pulsed through him. He tried to hold back, wanting to hold on to the moment. But he couldn't. Unable to do anything else, he began to move, faster, harder, driving them both until sensations overpowered and consumed them.

WHEN SHE COULD breathe again, J.C. discovered that she and Nik were lying face-to-face on the bed. His eyes were still closed and his hand was motionless at her waist—which was probably the only reason her brain cells were working.

Her eyes drifted over the thick, dark lashes, the stubble of his five o'clock shadow, then moved downward over the smooth muscles in his shoulders and arms. They were lying too close for her to get a good view of the rest of him; however, the image of him stripping naked had managed to indelibly imprint itself in her mind.

On a scale of one to ten, one being the Hunchback of Notre Dame and ten being Matt Damon in *The Bourne Identity,* Nik Angelis was about a twenty. With a lot of potential for increasing his score.

Which objectively speaking should be great for a sex buddy. Eye candy in a guy was always a bonus, right? And when looks were combined with style and expert technical ability—well, there was no way around it, she was a very lucky girl.

But somehow J.C. didn't think that the fun, palsy-walsy guy you invited over for no-strings, buddy sex should be someone who could set you off like a rocket every time he touched you. The article in *Cosmo* had listed several drawbacks to the sex-buddy scenario, but they hadn't mentioned that one. Or the danger of choosing a sex buddy you might get addicted to.

Of course, addictions took time to develop, J.C.

reminded herself. She and Nik were not going to be in this situation much longer. Their little affaire had "short term" written all over it. As soon as Snake Eyes was in custody and Nik's captain figured out what had happened at St. Peter's, she and Nik Angelis would go their separate ways. And in the meantime, well, she'd just have to get a handle on what it was about him that made her react like a...sex fiend.

Another thought occurred to her. There was always the possibility that they'd gotten each other out of their systems. As if to directly refute that theory, J.C. felt Nik's penis probing against her again. And her legs, traitors that they were, were already opening. One of them had even moved over his thigh to give him easier access.

But she would have moved back—she was almost sure of it—if he hadn't opened his eyes and tightened his grip on her waist. "Going somewhere?"

"I...no." She couldn't go anywhere, not when his fingers and those laser-blue eyes were sending fresh waves of heat through her.

He moved his hips forward, let her feel him growing harder. "Good."

She nearly protested when he released her waist and moved slightly away. Then she realized he was getting another condom from the nightstand.

"I'm not done with you yet."

"Good," she managed as he urged her onto her back and settled himself between her legs again.

He framed her face with his hands and brushed his lips over hers. "In fact, we're just getting started."

And Nik Angelis was a man who kept his word.

8

NIK PUT THE finishing touches to the sketch he'd made, then set down his marker and stepped back to survey his work. The whiteboard took up one wall of the small, eight-by-ten office in his apartment, and he'd used nearly all of it to draw a floor plan of St. Peter's Church, the rectory, the parking lot and the streets surrounding them.

This was his "thinking room," a place away from the station where he came to sift through the details of whatever case he was working on. If he couldn't walk through the crime scene in person, he could at least mentally walk through what had happened.

Opening a small cabinet, he turned on a CD player, punched the volume down to low and the soft sound of a jazz trombone filled the space. The room was furnished with only the bare essentials—a desk, a chair, a small sofa, because he often thought better when he was lying down—and an enlarged color photo on the wall of a seascape in Greece. His dad had brought the photo back from his recent trip, and Nik had asked for it and had it framed.

The photo helped him to think, too. Usually.

Nik took a long swallow of coffee. Trouble was, his thoughts kept returning to the woman who was sleeping in his bed. It hadn't been easy to leave her. There'd been that moment after he'd taken his shower when he'd wanted nothing more than to wake her and make love with her again. And he might have—no, he would have—if she hadn't looked so...*right* lying there. Just as she'd looked somehow *right* straightening his kitchen.

He didn't understand it. J.C. Riley was... Nik ran a hand through his hair. Hell, he didn't know what she was. How long had he known her? Five hours? Setting down his coffee, he began to pace in the small room.

Treat her like a case and review the facts, Angelis. Her father was the mayor, and everyone knew that Mayor Riley had married into money. His second wife's family owned Hansen Foods, whose products lined at least thirty percent of most grocery stores' shelves.

So J.C. Riley was a rich girl. On the other hand, she'd opened a catering business and seemed deter-·mined to make it a success. His father would like her, Nik thought. The success of his restaurant had always been very important to Spiro Angelis. And Nik knew that his father had suffered a great personal disappointment when none of his sons had wanted to take over The Poseidon.

What he knew from firsthand experience was that J.C. Riley enjoyed bossing people around. And she was very smart. She'd certainly picked up on the fact that he had a personal interest in figuring out what had happened at St. Peter's Church. Stuffing his hands in his pockets, Nik continued to pace. He wasn't comfortable with the fact that he was that transparent to her.

But there was no denying that for him this case was very personal. What he felt for Roman Oliver went beyond a sense of family obligation. Over the years since Kit had first brought him home, Nik had come to admire Roman as a man and to like him as a friend. He'd spoken nothing less than the truth to Roman's father. He was going to find out what happened.

He had to for both Roman's and J.C.'s sakes.

Pausing, he rested his hip on the edge of his desk and refocused his mind on J.C. She was rich, bossy, smart and on top of that, she had a curiosity that more than matched Alice's and probably led her down into just as many rabbit holes.

He frowned. Prime example—she'd rushed headlong into the sacristy after hearing gunfire, and now a man was hell-bent on killing her. The woman had more guts than brains. She needed a keeper.

And he'd been handpicked for the job.

Shit. A man would have to be crazy to think about getting seriously involved with a woman like that.

Nik stopped, stunned at the direction his thoughts had taken. No way. He was *not* thinking of getting involved with J.C. Riley. He'd already broken a rule by becoming "sex buddies" with someone he was supposed to be protecting. Wasn't that bad enough?

Nik reached for his coffee mug, found it empty and swore under his breath. He wasn't a man who made a habit of lying to himself. If he wasn't thinking of J.C. in more serious terms, why hadn't he stayed right beside her in that bed and continued to enjoy all the side benefits of being a sex buddy?

He ran a frustrated hand through his hair. What in the hell was he worried about anyway? Whatever was going on in his head, his relationship with J.C. Riley had "temporary" written all over it. They came from different worlds, they wanted different things. She didn't even like him, for heaven's sake. As soon as Snake Eyes was in custody, she'd go back to her life and he'd resume his.

And while he was stewing about this, her would-be killer was planning his next move. And the police were building their case against Roman Oliver.

Nik swore again, at himself this time. By some lucky twist of fate, she was still alive. If he wanted to keep her that way, he'd better stick to the plan and start doing his job. Easing a hip onto his desk, he picked up his recorder and focused his attention on his whiteboard.

J.C. WASN'T SURE how long she'd been standing and staring at Nik. She'd borrowed one of his shirts and followed the soft sounds of a jazz trombone from the bedroom to the doorway of a small office. She should have knocked immediately to signal her presence, but he'd been so intent on talking into the small recorder that she'd waited.

He was working. The realization did more to ease the hurt she'd felt when she'd awakened to find him gone than the lecture she'd given herself as she'd showered. She'd been foolish to think of his absence as a form of rejection. Clearly, she was going to have to work on the sex-buddy thing. Equally clear was the fact that he was having an easier time with the concept than she was.

His hair was still damp from a shower, just as hers was. Since he was standing with his back to her, she could look her fill. He was wearing nothing but jeans, low on the hips, leaving his back and feet bare. She tried to recall if she'd ever before found bare feet sexy. He ran one of his hands through his hair, and she recalled just how that hand had felt on her skin. Heat pooled in her center.

That was all it took. He didn't even have to touch her to make her desire him all over again. She wanted to walk in there right now, wrap her arms around him and feel that hard body pressed against hers. The urge to do just that was nearly overpowering.

Get a grip, J.C. Breathe. No, that wasn't going to work. She'd used his soap and shampoo, and the scent was…him.

Think. Someone was trying to kill her. It would be a lot smarter and safer to concentrate on that. Deliberately, she switched her gaze to the other objects in the room. It was sparsely furnished, and it reminded her of the small office she used in her apartment. No window, no distractions. She had a couch, too, but her computer was a laptop. Her choice of work music was different, too. She preferred the classics—Galway on the flute, Bell on the violin…

And instead of a whiteboard, she'd lined one wall with cork where she pinned up her current research and ideas for new recipes. Narrowing her eyes, J.C. studied Nik's whiteboard more closely and recognized the sketch of the crime scene. For the first time, her brain registered what he was saying into the recorder.

"…witness saw five people enter through the sacristy door. The bride and the mystery blonde, the groom and his driver/bodyguard. And Roman Oliver. She didn't see the shooter she calls Snake Eyes come in that way. Nor did she see Sadie Oliver, the bride's older sister. So they must have entered through the main doors in the vestibule."

"Someone must have let Snake Eyes in. I'm not sure about this Sadie Oliver. Who's she?"

Nik whirled to face her as she entered the room. "I'm working."

She lifted an eyebrow. "I can see that. You're trying to figure out what happened at the church and why. Your captain wouldn't approve. But I do. Let me help you."

Nik's eyes narrowed. "I work better alone."

"So do I. But I have a vested interest in this. I want my life back." Her eyes narrowed. "And I think you have a vested interest in this, too, aside from babysitting me. It has something to do with your brother Kit, doesn't it? When I asked you before, you said, 'Maybe.'" She folded her arms across her chest. "What's Kit's involvement in all of this?"

Nik opened his mouth and the look in his eyes had her temper flaring. "Don't you dare give me that speech about how you're the cop and you're the one who gives the orders. I think we've gotten beyond that. And I…" She let the sentence trail off when his lips twitched.

"What?" she asked.

"Fair is fair. If I have to stop giving orders, so do you. Deal?"

It was her own lips that were twitching now. "Maybe. But first, you have to tell me what your special interest in this case is."

When Nik had finished telling her about Kit's relationship with Roman Oliver and the case that the police were building against Roman, she moved to him, wrapped her arms around him and said, "I'm sorry. What can I do to help?"

Nik felt surprise and something else move through him—not the passion that he'd felt before. This was different, warm and sweet. And when he put his arms around her, it just felt right.

J.C. was the one who drew back, and when she did, she was all business as she turned to study his whiteboard. "We'll just have to figure out what happened at the church."

Had she felt what he'd just felt, he wondered. He wanted to take her back in his arms and ask her. But ask her what? He wasn't even sure of his own feelings. How could he ask her what hers were?

"When I arrived, Father Mike let me into the rectory. Then he went across the walkway and let himself into the church. So the church was locked up until then."

"How can you be sure that he didn't open the front doors?"

"I can't, but think about it. There weren't any guests invited to this wedding. The bride and the groom and even your friend Roman all came in through the back. They either knew that Father Mike wasn't opening the doors or they tried them, found them locked and drove around."

She tapped a finger on the area he'd labeled "parking lot." "The dining room of the rectory has a full view of this area. If Snake Eyes had come in through the sacristy entrance, I would have seen him. I saw everybody else. Therefore, I'm betting someone had to have let him in. Same goes for Sadie Oliver." She turned to face Nik. "Who is she, by the way?"

"The bride's older sister. She's a tall brunette and she left her purse in the vestibule near the spot where I found Roman."

"So she's missing, too?"

"Yes. But let's get back to Snake Eyes. If your theory is correct, he must have had an inside man."

"Or woman," J.C. said.

"You're thinking of the mystery blonde?"

"She's a possibility."

He nodded. "But right now Roman is the prime suspect."

"But he's a victim, too," J.C. pointed out.

Nik shrugged. "He could have planned it that way or it could have happened by accident. The police are going to figure *him* for the inside man."

She turned to him. "How do you know what the police are figuring?"

"It's what I would be thinking myself if I hadn't known Roman for over ten years. He was Kit's roommate in college. He's been coming to the restaurant and our house since he was eighteen. He's got a temper, yes, but he's a grown man, and he's learned how to control it. I can see him coming there to stop the wedding. Hell, they're kids. But I can't see him bringing accomplices with orders to kill the priest." He frowned at the whiteboard. "And my relationship to him, my feelings, make me less than objective."

"No problem. I can be objective for both of us. There's no way Roman Oliver let the shooter in. The argument began within seconds of his arrival, and after that, I'd say he was busy in the sacristy."

Nik studied her. "You're sure?"

She nodded. "I'll even put it in writing for your captain, if you like." Then she shot him a grin. "I told you I could help you, Slick. What do we do next?"

"We figure out who did let Snake Eyes in. What about Father Mike?"

J.C. considered that for a moment, then shook her head. "Father Mike was very concerned about keeping the wedding a secret. No one was supposed to be there besides the bride and groom and two witnesses. If someone had knocked on a door, he would have told them to go away."

"Unless Father Mike was the inside man."

"No way." There was triumph in the look she shot him. "If Father Mike was in on it, why would Snake Eyes try to kill him?"

She had a quick mind. Nik made a mental note to add that to the list of things he was learning about J.C. Riley. He preferred to work alone, but she *was* helping him, and he'd never been a man to cut off his nose to spite his face.

Moving closer to the sketch, he pointed to the two other entrances—the main doors at the front of the church and one off the room where baptisms were performed that allowed access from the side street. "Which door do you think Snake Eyes came in?"

Without hesitating, J.C. pointed to the front entrance. "That one."

"Why not the side door?" Nik asked.

"Not many people know about it. And Father Mike

uses that room when he's setting up a wedding. He'd be sure to see if the door was left ajar. If you wanted to let someone in unnoticed, a much better plan would be to open one of the main doors in the vestibule and leave it ajar. The person could slip in whenever they arrived."

Nik considered her theory and decided he liked it. "So Snake Eyes could slip in and if the door was still open, Sadie Oliver got in that way, too. That would explain why she didn't have to use the sacristy door like everyone else."

"My pick for the inside man is the man who got shot, the one I figured was a driver/bodyguard."

Nik stared at her. She was ahead of him on that one. "How so?"

She kept her eyes on the whiteboard. "The argument and the fight took place in the sacristy. We both think Roman came to stop the wedding. He and Paulo got into a fight."

Nik's cell phone rang. He pulled it out and flipped it open. "Hold that thought."

"I've got some bad news." Dinah's voice was pitched low and he could hear the noises of the squad room in the background.

His stomach knotted. "Roman?"

"No further word on him yet. But the dead man in the sacristy has been identified as Paulo Carlucci's bodyguard, Gino DeLucca. The bullet that killed him probably came from Roman's gun. They're still running tests to confirm that, but I thought you'd want to know."

"Thanks. Any news on the man who shot Father Mike?"

"Not yet."

Nik tucked his phone into his pocket. "No news on Snake Eyes."

"Is Roman all right?" J.C. asked.

"No news on him, either."

"But...?" She moved forward to take his hand. "There's a 'but' in there. Tell me."

She saw a lot, and she cared. He was a bit uncomfortable with the emotions that were stirring in him. "My partner says that ballistics will most likely confirm that a bullet from Roman's gun killed the man in the sacristy. And you were right about that. The dead man was Paulo Carlucci's bodyguard, Gino DeLucca."

"Then it makes sense that he was the inside man. He came to the church with Paulo. If Father Mike had them come earlier for a rehearsal, he would have been able to case the place. He also probably knew that Juliana and Paulo were seeing each other. He could have leaked the information. Maybe to Snake Eyes—whoever he is."

"The most likely person he'd leak it to would be someone in the Carlucci family."

Together, they turned and looked at the whiteboard again.

"Paulo and Roman are busy trying to beat each other up," Nik said, picturing it in his mind. "Father Mike is probably trying to break the fight up. And DeLucca slips away to let the killer in. Or maybe that's what he's doing when the fight breaks out. Then he comes back to the sacristy. Maybe his job is to keep the groom out of it while Snake Eyes handles the priest."

"Or the bride," J.C. commented.

"Could be," Nik mused. "And since we're assuming

that Roman's not part of it, his presence must have been a surprise."

"And not a happy one," J.C. said. "Roman could have shot DeLucca in self-defense. Then he tells Paulo to run. I heard someone tell Paulo that after the shots. Paulo races up the sacristy stairs to the loft to protect his bride." She used her finger to trace a path from the altar, down the center aisle of the church to the vestibule. "Roman follows Snake Eyes, chases him up the vestibule stairs, they struggle and Roman falls." She paused and frowned as she brought her finger back to the altar. "Then Snake Eyes comes all the way back to the altar to shoot Father Mike? He would have had to really work fast. And there were those shots I heard coming from the choir loft when Snake Eyes was at the altar."

Nik studied the sketch. She was making sense. "So maybe Gino DeLucca let more than one person in."

"Or he left the door open and someone took advantage of it."

For a moment, neither of them said a thing. Nik tried to think with his cop's mind. "On the other hand, if we go along with the current police theory that Roman was behind everything and brought backup, they sure as hell didn't come in the sacristy door with him, and when would he have had time to go all the way to the vestibule to let them in?"

"He wouldn't have."

"That's what I want to believe. But a good cop doesn't play favorites." He shook his head. "I just can't conceive of the man I know coming to his sister's wedding to stop it with armed gunmen. I could never do that to Philly, and I don't believe Roman could do it, either."

J.C. slipped her hand into his. After a moment, he said, "Whichever way you look at it, whoever was behind it, the plan went wrong. And it all happened so fast. When did Father Mike let you in the church?"

"Six forty-five. It was five to seven when the groom arrived, a few minutes later when the bride and the mystery blonde went in. Roman arrived shortly after seven."

"I got the call from dispatch at seven-twelve." Nik moved closer to the board. "There were shots fired in that upstairs room. There was blood in two different areas. Based on the timing of the shots you heard from the sacristy, I think you're right, and Snake Eyes must have had an accomplice in addition to DeLucca and that's who Roman chased up the stairs. Meanwhile Snake Eyes's job was to eliminate the priest."

"What about the mystery blonde?"

For a moment neither of them spoke. Then J.C. said, "Maybe she's the accomplice who fired the shot in the upstairs room and pushed Roman down the stairs. Then she takes off with the bride and groom, and Snake Eyes stays behind to eliminate witnesses."

Nik's eyes narrowed as he turned the possibility over in his mind. "You're thinking it was a kidnapping plot?"

"It's possible, isn't it? The bride and groom have disappeared. Their families would pay a lot to get them back."

"Sadie Oliver has also disappeared."

"You think she was kidnapped, too?" J.C. asked.

"Or she did the kidnapping." His thumbs were pricking big time, but he wasn't sure at which possibility. "There's still a lot we don't know."

"Right." She cocked her head to the side as she studied the whiteboard. "It's kind of like a recipe."

Nik turned to look at her. "How's that?"

"We're still lacking some of the key ingredients and the proper amounts. But once we have them, it will all make—"

Her sentence was interrupted by a growling sound.

"What in hell is that?" Nik asked with a frown.

J.C. pressed a hand against her stomach. "I'm hungry."

"Again?"

She lifted her chin. "Still. I was hungry when we got here, remember? And your cupboards were bare."

"If you have to eat all the time, why aren't you fat?"

"I work out and I keep moving."

"Yeah." He grinned at her. "I noticed. And I'm not complaining." He leaned closer and kissed her.

She was just leaning in to him when he drew back and led the way out of the room. "As it happens, I'm hungry, too."

Her stomach growled again. "If you're calling out, I like my pizza loaded. If they offer anchovies—"

"It's after midnight, a little late for deliveries."

She caught up to him at the door. "Wait. If you're going out for fast food, I'll come with you."

He shot her a horrified look. "You're a caterer and you eat fast food?"

J.C. lifted her chin. "I have eclectic tastes. Besides, I get hungry a lot."

He lifted both hands palms out. "I'm not criticizing. But I think between us, we can do better than fast food. I used to cook in my father's restaurant, and I make a mean omelet."

She cocked an eyebrow. "So do I, but not without eggs."

Nik laughed, and the rich sound of it filling the air made her smile.

"I'm going to borrow some food from my aunt," he said as he reached for the doorknob. "I'll be right back."

"Get some cheese, too," she said. "And tomatoes and onions if she has any. Parsley would be good—and basil."

"Oregano is what you need for the perfect omelet."

"Maybe I should come with you."

"No." He blocked her when she reached the door, his expression suddenly sober. "I want you to stay here until I get back and lock the door behind me."

Her eyes widened. "Do you think someone followed us here?"

"No, but I didn't think your pal Snake Eyes would shoot at you in the parking lot with all us cops around, either. So I'm not taking any chances."

J.C.'s stomach sank.

He must have read her expression because he leaned down and kissed her again. It was exactly the kind of kiss a person might get from a buddy. Quick. Friendly. Intellectually, she got it, but her knees betrayed her and turned to jelly. She barely kept herself from leaning in to him.

"Not to worry, Pipsqueak. He's not going to get past me. In the meantime, relax and conserve your energy so that we can fight about who gets to make the omelet when I get back."

9

J.C. STARED DOWN at the bag of groceries Nik had just handed her through the door. He was just outside talking to Kit. She knew because she'd ignored what he'd said and had opened the door to check on him. He hadn't been more than ten feet away, deep in conversation with his brother.

So why was she feeling so…? What? Ever since he'd left, not more than five minutes ago, she'd felt…odd.

Frowning, she whirled and carried the bag into the kitchen. He hadn't been gone more than three minutes when she'd decided to go find him. And not because she was frightened. Oh, that might have been the lie she told herself. But it wasn't true. What she'd felt when Nik had left the apartment was…something else.

Loneliness?

No. She definitely wasn't feeling lonely. Annoyed with herself, she unpacked the bag, stuffing eggs, cream, butter and cheese into the refrigerator and then placing onions and tomatoes into hanging wire baskets. She never felt lonely. Growing up in a large family sort of prevented that. It hadn't mattered that she was the only girl. Her younger brothers had treated her just like one of the guys. And she hadn't felt lonely when she'd moved into her own apartment. In fact, she'd enjoyed the solitude.

She paused while lifting a skillet out of a cupboard. She couldn't be missing Nik. That was ridiculous. But hadn't she felt a surge of relief when she'd seen him at the head of the stairs talking to Kit?

J.C. turned away from the stove and strode back into the living room. What she was feeling was definitely not the reaction a woman should have to a pal she was just having sex with.

Think of other things, Jude Catherine. There's a killer after you so coming up with a plan would be good. She strode into Nik's small office and found a pencil and a pad. Returning to the living room, she sat on the couch, tucked her feet under her and began to write. First thing in the morning, she and Nik were going to the police station so that she could look at mug shots. Parker had been insistent about that. Tonight, Nik's captain and her godfather wanted her to rest and recover from the gunshot wound.

Lifting Nik's shirt, she glanced at the bandage that covered her upper arm. It was throbbing a little, but it looked fine. Truth be told, she hadn't thought about it at all while she and Nik had been making love. And it certainly hadn't impeded them in any way. Nothing had seemed to impede them, she recalled with a smile.

Then she forced the smile away. Not a good thing to be thinking about, Jude Catherine. She might not be an expert on Buddy sex, but she didn't think having it should lead to feelings of loneliness; nor should it fuel fantasies of having more of the same.

J.C. was refocusing her attention on her list when a phone rang. It rang two more times before she located Nik's cell phone where he'd left it along with his gun on the bookcase. She hesitated only a second before reaching for it. It could be the hospital—or news about Snake Eyes.

"Hello?"

"Jude Catherine, is that you?"

"Daddy?"

"Where are you? Are you all right? I've been worried sick about you."

J.C. closed her eyes and prayed for patience. "I'm fine."

"Captain Parker tells me that you were shot. He assigned his so-called best man, and this officer let someone put a bullet in you."

J.C. rose to her feet. "He didn't let someone put a bullet in me and it's only a—"

"Don't interrupt me, Jude Catherine. And for once in your life, don't argue. Obviously, the officer assigned to you is incompetent. You can tell him I've made arrangements to—"

"He's not an officer. He's Detective Nik Angelis, and he *is not* incompetent." J.C. heard her voice rising, so she paused to take a deep breath.

"I disagree."

J.C. pressed a hand to her temple. She and her father frequently disagreed, and yelling at him was not the best way to handle him.

"I've already told Captain Parker to fire Angelis from the job of bodyguard."

"You can't fire him," J.C. shouted into the phone.

"Now, calm down, sweetheart. I know what's best for you."

She felt anger and frustration roll through her. He always thought he knew what was best.

"I've hired a private security firm, Rossi Investigations, and they're going to take over. One of the men they've assigned to you used to be a CIA agent. All you have to do is tell me where you are and they'll be there as soon as they can. I promise you, sweetheart—you're going to be safe."

Summoning up all the calm she could find, J.C. said, "I'm not going to tell you where I am." Then she held the phone away from her ear so that she didn't have to listen to her father's tirade. He'd run down eventually, and then maybe she could make him really listen.

Suddenly, the phone was taken out of her hand. She whirled to find Nik standing right behind her. How long had he been there? How much had he heard?

"Mayor Riley, this is Nik Angelis. I think we should talk."

"Put my daughter back on the phone."

Nik was standing a few feet away from her, but her father's voice carried clearly.

"Not just yet. First, we need to straighten out a few things." He took her hand and drew her to the couch. Her father continued to talk as they settled themselves on it. Nik kept her hand in his, and she made no attempt to pull hers free.

When her father finally finished, Nik said, "I share all of your concerns about the safety of your daughter, sir. And I promise you I'm going to keep her safe. But

I'm not going to turn her over to the men from Rossi Investigations."

J.C.'s gaze flew to Nik's face. He was being very patient with her father. He'd yet to raise his voice. But there was a tension in the set of his jaw and even in the way he held her hand that told her he wasn't nearly as calm as he sounded.

"What do you mean you're not going to turn her over? I'm told they're the best security firm in the city."

"I agree. They're small, but they deserve their reputation. I went to UC Berkeley with Luke Rossi. I can vouch for him personally. And the ex-CIA agent you mentioned—that would be Cole Buchanan?"

There was a pause on the other end of the line. Then Mayor Riley said, "If you know this firm and agree that they're the best, why are you refusing to turn my daughter over to them?"

"I have several reasons." He met J.C.'s eyes. "Top of the list is I never walk away from a job once I start it."

J.C. felt some of her own tension ease.

"I can have your captain call you in and reassign you."

"Actually, you can't, sir. Officially, I'm on vacation this weekend. I'm supposed to be fishing and sailing with my brothers. And I've only given you the reason that's at the top of *my* list. What should be at the top of *yours* is that J.C. doesn't want to be turned over to a security firm. Right now she and I are getting along and she's cooperating fully. What do you think her attitude will be if you force a new bodyguard on her, one she doesn't want?"

There was another silence on the other end of the

phone. J.C. felt admiration surge through her. He was making her father think. Patrick Riley was a reasonable man when he could rein in his temper and emotions.

"She'll give them a hard time."

"I see you know your daughter, sir."

To J.C.'s astonishment, the booming sound of her father's laughter filled the air. "So, it seems, do you."

"She may even try to get away from them. I couldn't allow that to happen. So I'm not turning her over."

Another pause and then, "Yes…yes, I can see your concern."

"I promise you, sir, I'm not going to let the bastard get another shot at her. You have my word on that. And if it will make you feel any better, if I feel the need for backup, I'll call Cole Buchanan at Rossi Investigations. I have the number."

There was a brief silence on the other end of the line.

Please, Daddy, she prayed silently.

Finally, her father said, "Good. For now, I'll settle for that." There was another pause. "How is she?"

J.C. could see the tension drain out of Nik, and she felt her own anxiety fading.

"I'll let her tell you, sir."

J.C. took the phone, but she kept her eyes on Nik. "What I am is hungry, and Detective Angelis has promised me an omelet."

Her father laughed again. "Take care, little girl. I love you."

"I love you, too, Dad."

Nik took the phone and set it on the coffee table. He thought of how she'd looked when he'd come into the room—furious, her back ramrod-straight. She'd reminded him of a Greek warrior goddess about to throw a lightning bolt. And yet beneath that bravado was a vulnerability that she didn't let show too often. Was that why he'd felt such an overwhelming need to rush to her defense and protect her?

Angling his head to one side, he continued to study her. No other woman had ever made him feel quite that way. Unless they were family. And now, sitting on the couch with him, she looked suddenly tired. Why hadn't he noticed that before?

"Did Kit have any news about Roman?" she asked.

"Nothing that I didn't find out at the hospital. He has a skull fracture that the doctors believe poses less of a threat than the swelling at the base of his spine. If it doesn't go down by tomorrow, they're going to operate. In the meantime, the doctors are keeping him sedated, and they won't allow any visitors. Not even his family."

"I'm so sorry, Nik."

"If he could talk to someone, he could fill in a lot of the blanks and help us to figure out what happened."

J.C. took his hand. "You're going to find out what happened, and you'll clear his name."

"Yes." Nik wondered if the similar assurances he'd given to his brother had been as comforting.

Lifting her hand, he noted how small it was, how delicate her wrist was. Lowering his head, he brushed his lips over her knuckles and watched her eyes darken.

Then she cleared her throat. "You handled Dad beautifully. I never have that much patience."

"You have to handle him more often than I do. I'm sure I'd have my breaking point. Is he always that... bossy?"

She sighed as she nodded. "He loves me, but he wants to control my life."

Nik thought about that. The moment he'd learned who she was, he'd jumped to the conclusion that she'd been spoiled and pampered. Maybe she'd been pampered, but he doubted she'd been spoiled. He was beginning to understand she'd had to struggle to become the person she was. Looking at her now and really seeing her, he felt something much quieter and richer than desire move through him.

"Don't get me wrong. Dad's a good man. But that's the way he is with all of us—domineering and overprotective. He likes to run the show and give the orders."

Nik bit back a smile. "I wondered where you'd gotten that from."

She narrowed her eyes. "I'm going to ignore that comment, but I'm not going to forget it."

"Heaven forbid."

She cocked her head to one side. "He offered you an out. You didn't want the job of guarding me. You could have turned me over to this ex-CIA agent and worked on the case to save your brother's friend."

He met her eyes steadily. "No, I couldn't have. What I said to your father is true. I don't walk away from a job once I start it. And besides, I like the Rossis and I wanted to protect them. You would have given them a terrible time."

Her chin lifted. "Yes. I would have."

With his free hand, Nik traced a finger along her jawline. "I haven't given you an easy time of it." He didn't as a rule manhandle women, and he wasn't at all comfortable with the sliver of guilt moving through him. He hadn't even been gentle with her when they'd been making love.

A little frown appeared on her forehead. "Why should you? You were just doing your job."

He slid one hand behind her neck and urged her closer. "This isn't part of my job." Then he brushed his lips softly against hers. Her sigh, and the way she moved closer, had desire sparking hot and wild inside of him. But he was going to go slow this time.

Drawing back, he said, "You're tired."

"No. Well…maybe a little."

Leaning in to her again, he began to tease her mouth with his, murmuring, "Maybe we ought to give each other a rain check on that omelet." He slipped his tongue between her lips for a taste. Her flavor nearly broke his resolve.

"Nik?"

"Shhh," he whispered. He ran a hand through the tumble of rich, red curls that were still damp. "So soft. It looks as though it should feel hot, but it doesn't."

She cleared her throat. "If we're not going to eat, we should go into your study and—"

"First things first," he murmured. Lifting her onto his lap, he kissed her eyes shut, then moved his mouth over her cheeks, along her jaw and finally down to the pulse that beat slow and thick at the base of her throat.

"You want to make love again."

"Ever since we stopped making love the last time. This time I'm going to taste you. All over. Starting here." Nik sank his teeth into her earlobe and whispered, "Any objections?"

"Shouldn't we—"

"You talk too much." Keeping his eyes on hers, he returned to her mouth, testing, teasing. "I think a little break is in order." He nipped her bottom lip, then soothed it with his tongue. He unbuttoned the shirt she was wearing and drew it down until it trapped her arms. Struggling against the urge to rush, he turned his attention to her throat.

J.C. arched her neck back to give him more access. She felt weak. Deliciously so. Her arms weren't trapped—not really—but they felt heavy. She wondered if she could lift them. But why would she want to when his mouth—so clever, so skillful—was sending ripples of fire and ice along her nerve endings.

She felt the moist warmth of his tongue tracing along her collarbone, and quivered. He brushed his lips over the tops of her breasts and then between them. Her nipples grew tight, hard, but he continued to move his mouth lower. J.C. sighed. "Nik?"

"Shhh. No orders this time. Just give yourself to me."

She felt the whisper of his breath right down to her toes and she could feel herself melting, floating. Helpless to do anything else, she arched back and gave herself over to the sensations. There were so many to absorb—the brush of his lips over her ribs, the scratch of his cheek against her skin, the wet heat of his tongue as it moved lower and lower down her stomach. He lingered at her waist as if there was some flavor there that he couldn't get enough of.

Time spun out, and the melting warmth inside of her simmered and threatened to boil. When he finally shifted her off of him and settled her on the couch, she clutched for him. Evading her hands, he stood to shed his clothes.

Now, she thought. Surely he would take her now, fill that aching inside of her. But he surprised her again by kneeling down in front of her and spreading her thighs apart.

She lay her hands on his where they rested just above her knees. "I want you. Please."

He met her eyes and said, "All of you, remember? I'm going to taste all of you first."

He began by moving down the length of her thigh, over her knee and calf to her ankle. Nik lingered there, using his mouth and tongue on her feet. She was a feast, and he wanted more. He shifted his attention to her other leg. There was such a lush warmth here, a light coolness there. Her pulse pounded harder there, stuttered here. And every time her breath hitched, every time she moaned his name, his own blood pounded through him.

Unable to wait any longer, he cruised his mouth up her inner thigh and took an intoxicating taste of the pink nub at her center. She was like a fine wine and just as seductive.

J.C. cried out and arched, calling his name. He kept his mouth pressed to her as she rode out the wave of her climax. Then he carefully drew her to the floor, sheathed himself in the condom and found his place between her legs.

"Jude Catherine."

She opened her eyes and saw only him. The candlelight shone on the hard planes and angles of his face. His eyes were dark, almost black like his hair. In that moment, she knew she was his. And she wanted him mindlessly. She reached out to him. "Nik, please."

As if he were waiting only for that, he slipped inside of her. His hands found hers, linked, and then he began to rock against her. Even then he moved slowly, kindling the heat inside of her again and building it. She wanted to hold on to the moment, hold on to to him. And she did as he quickened the pace, slowly, surely until the heat burst into flames and consumed them both.

Afterward, they lay together, their arms wrapped around each other, for a long time.

10

NIK LEANED on the horn until the van in front of him moved, then began to nose his car into the left-hand turn lane.

"You shouldn't drive while you're angry," J.C. said. "We could have grabbed a bite at the diner across from the police station."

Nik negotiated the turn, then slammed on his brakes as he found himself in yet another lane of cars that was barely moving. "I'm not angry."

"Right. And you're not trying to kill us by the way you're driving."

Nik barely kept from swearing. "I'm just frustrated because things are looking worse for Roman Oliver." That was the understatement of the year. The case against Roman was becoming more solid by the minute.

While J.C. had been looking at mug shots, Dinah had filled him in on what she knew. Both the Olivers and the Carluccis had received ransom notes, demanding money for the return of Paulo and Juliana. No mention of Sadie. So that pretty well shot his theory that Sadie had been taken along with the bride and groom. And it strengthened the theory that Sadie and Roman had been working together, that the kidnapping had been part of their plan, and that Sadie had carried through with it after Roman was hurt. The ransom notes demanding five million for the return of the bride and five million for the return of the groom were their motive. That kind of cash could clinch the land deal that they were vying with the Carluccis for.

"I know the ransom notes look bad for your friend, Roman," J.C. said.

He turned to stare at her. "How did you hear about the ransom notes? No one is supposed to know about them." Parker was keeping a very tight lid on it, and his captain wouldn't like it if he learned that Dinah had told him. If word was spreading that quickly, it would be headline news by the end of the day.

"I overheard you and Dinah talking. I have good ears, and looking at those mug shots was boring. There's got to be an explanation. Roman wouldn't kidnap his own sister."

"The line of reasoning is that he had to kidnap both the bride and the groom to deflect suspicion from himself."

"And they think his sister Sadie helped him?"

"Dammit. Did you eavesdrop on everything Dinah and I said?" Seeing his chance, he jammed his foot on the accelerator and shot the car into the next lane.

"See? You are angry with me. Why don't you just admit it? You're mad because I couldn't identify Snake Eyes in any of the mug shots I looked at this morning. I can understand your frustration. But he just wasn't there."

Nik shot her another glance. She was staring straight ahead with her hands clasped tightly in her lap. Cursing himself, he drew in a deep breath. "I'm not angry with you." He heartily wished it was anger that had sunk its claws into his gut and not fear. And the fear had nothing to do with the case. He could keep her safe. But in the early morning light as he'd watched her sleep beside him in his bed, he'd realized that he could no longer keep himself safe from her.

She'd gotten to him. Some time during the night, he'd lost something of himself to her. That had never happened to him before and it had been gnawing away at him all morning.

She mumbled something.

Liar. He let the word hang in the air between them. If she wanted to believe he was angry with her, fine. Hadn't he spent most of the morning trying to convince himself that they'd both be wise to back off a bit? So why didn't he just tell her that instead of driving like a…fiend?

Slamming on the brakes, he managed to avoid smashing into the bumper of the car in front of him. Barely. The truth was as much as he might want to back off from J.C. Riley, he couldn't. From the moment that she'd stepped out of that closet in the sacristy, her hair mussed, those green eyes wide with fear, she'd bewitched him. He felt as if he'd been sucked into a whirlpool and he was very much afraid that he couldn't break free.

Could she be right? Was he angry with her for that?

"Stop the car," J.C. said.

Nik shot her a look. "It's as good as stopped. You might have noticed that this traffic's moving at a snail's pace."

She lifted her chin. "I mean stop as in park the car. I'm hungry."

"There's news." He turned his attention back to the road. "Sit tight. It's only two more blocks to the food."

"It could take hours to get there. If you'd tell me where you're headed, maybe I could think of an alternate route. As a caterer, I'm pretty good at getting places fast."

Nik glanced at her again. "And you think a cop isn't?"

"Look, Ghirardelli Square is right over there. Let me run in. I want chocolate."

"There'll be no running in. I told you at the station, I'm taking you to a place where I know you'll be safe."

J.C. BIT DOWN on her lip to stop her reply. Safe? That was a laugh. The truth was, she wasn't safe—not from Nik Angelis. The fear that had been fluttering around in her stomach all morning settled into a hard little ball.

Ever since she'd woken up this morning, Nik had been keeping his distance. Oh, he'd been polite enough. Kind, too. He'd had an omelet waiting for her in the kitchen when she'd gotten out of the shower. But he'd made phone calls while she'd eaten. And he'd barely spoken to her on the way to the police station. In short, he was being the perfect sex buddy. She wondered if he was this way with every woman he slept with.

No, she wasn't going to go there. She didn't want to think that Nik had spent a night like last night with any other woman. J.C. bit back a sigh.

She couldn't have imagined what had happened during the night. Though it hurt her now to look at him, she did. Damn him. There'd been moments during the night when he'd been hers. What had happened between them had been more than just sex. Hadn't it?

Not that it mattered now, because he was clearly backing off. Maybe he was even dumping her. Turning, she stared blindly out the windshield. Rejection always hurt. But she'd handled it before, hadn't she? As she glanced at him, a little flame of anger began to build inside of her. Well, two could play that game. He wasn't the only one who could back off.

Nik blasted his horn and nearly kissed the fender of a car as he shot his to the curb. "This is it."

J.C. glanced out the window. The letters on the re-volving glass door read The Poseidon. It looked like other restaurants that she'd seen, and she wondered what it was about this one that made Nik think he could keep her safe here.

Nik tossed his key to a waiting valet as he opened her door. "Park it in the alley, Cato."

"Sure thing."

She stared at the tall, handsome man who was cir-cling the car as Nik pulled her into the revolving doors. "He's nearly as handsome as you are, Slick."

She felt his grip tighten on her arm. Score one for her.

The room they stepped into was large and airy. Directly behind the empty hostess desk was a glass window that offered a view of the Golden Gate Bridge. A velvet rope closed off the stairs that led to the upper level. J.C. caught a glimpse of white tablecloths and silver candlesticks before her attention was captured by the music and general hubbub rising from the restau-rant on the lower level. The bar was mahogany, the walls behind it brick with fishing nets strung across it. Servers moved swiftly between tables crowded with customers. Through an archway, she could see plants, more tables and a dance floor.

"We'll have to wait for a table here." She shot Nik a narrow-eyed glance. "Some chocolate would have tided me over."

Before he had a chance to reply, a young woman appeared at the top of the stairs and flew toward them.

"Nik!" She wrapped her arms around him and hugged him hard. J.C. figured the young woman had to be Nik's sister. She had the same brown eyes and curly dark hair. But she was much shorter and had the face of a pixie. J.C. suddenly realized that Nik had brought her to his family's restaurant.

"Hi." With a smile, J.C. extended her hand. "I'm J.C. Riley, and you've got to be Nik's sister."

"I hope you won't hold that against me. I'm Philly." She squeezed J.C.'s hand. "Welcome to The Poseidon."

"He tells me that you have a special way to communicate with animals."

"Really?" Philly shot a look at Nik and he shrugged. "He's usually not a blabbermouth."

"I think it's so cool. I'd love to talk to you about it sometime. Unless you don't want to."

"Why not?"

"Well, some people think that psychics are sort of, you know—woo-woo. But I don't. Really. I'm fascinated by it."

Philly grinned at her. "Wait until you meet Aunt Cass. She's the true psychic in the family. Is this your first visit to The Poseidon?"

J.C. nodded. "Yes, and I think I'm falling in love." She moved with Philly to the railing that looked out over the lower level. "I've always dreamed of owning a place like this—not Greek, of course, but a place where the food brings people in and builds a kind of community."

Philly laughed. "Well, you've picked a day to visit when the community is a bit shaky. Helena, our five-star chef, hasn't shown up yet, and Dad is worried. Has Nik told you about our father's midlife crisis?"

Nik watched J.C. shake her head. That was all it took for Philly to launch into the story of how six months ago their father had taken a trip back to Greece and had returned with the beautiful Helena, a renowned chef to help him expand the restaurant. The way Philly told it, their father sounded like Paris stealing Helen away to Troy. Any minute now a hollow wooden horse would make an appearance.

J.C. threw back her head and laughed when Philly explained how since she'd arrived, Helena had seized total creative control of the fine dining level, and she and their father Spiro had become rivals, each competing to create bigger and better dishes.

"So you've got your own version of *Iron Chef* going on," J.C. commented.

"Exactly! It makes for very high drama."

After that, Nik lost track of the story because all he could do was stare at J.C. The sun pouring in through the window had turned her hair to flames. She was beautiful. Why hadn't he noticed that before? And she looked so right standing there. He hadn't expected her to. Hadn't wanted her to. Hadn't he brought her here to convince himself that she couldn't possibly fit in with his life, with his family?

But she did fit in. Fear tightened in his stomach. Maybe he was just going to have to learn to live with that.

"Aunt Cass and I think that the real reason Dad invited Helena to come to San Francisco was because he fell in love with her, and we think that's the real reason that she came. But then something happened. Maybe my father got cold feet. For some reason the Angelis men seem to do that. My grandfather told me once that if he hadn't arranged for my father to come to this country, he probably never would have had the courage to come here on his own even though he was crazy in love with my mother. It was one of those love-at-first-sight deals. They met on a beach in Greece and that was it. It was the same way for my uncle Demetrius and Aunt Cass. I'm beginning to wonder if the family shouldn't do an intervention."

As if that was his cue, Nik watched his father appear at the head of the stairs. "Philly, has Helena called in yet?"

"No, Dad. You asked me that not five minutes ago."

"And who is this?" Spiro was staring at J.C. as he strode forward.

"This is J.C. Riley," Nik said.

"It's a pleasure, Ms. Riley." Spiro took her hand in both of his. "Spiro Angelis. Your name is familiar. You're in the catering business, right? Have an Affair with J.C. Riley, right?"

"How did you know?" J.C. asked.

Spiro beamed a smile at her. "I'm encouraging Helena to expand into catering—fancy stuff like weddings—and one of my distributors mentioned your name. He spoke very highly of you, but he failed to mention how beautiful you are."

Nik took J.C.'s arm.

"Ms. Riley is with you?"

The look his father sent him was all innocence.

"I'm with Nik but I'm not his date," J.C. said. "I'm his job. That's the extent of our relationship."

Nik felt the pain sting an area near his heart as surely as if she'd thrown a dart at him. She was backing off from him. Well, he'd just see about that.

"That doesn't change the fact that she's with me." J.C. jerked her arm, but he held it in a firm grip. "And she's going to stay with me. She was just telling Philly how much she loves the restaurant."

Spiro beamed again at J.C. "You're a woman of discerning taste. You're not Greek, are you?"

Smiling, J.C. shook her head. "Sorry."

"Aren't you needed at the bar?" Nik asked his father.

Just then the phone on the hostess desk rang, and Philly rushed to pick it up. A moment later, she said to her father, "Helena's here. She came in the back way, and she's at the bar."

Without another word, Spiro whirled and raced down the stairs.

"Drama," Philly said to J.C. and Nik. "Drama, drama, drama." She was laughing as she scanned the book on the hostess desk. "We're booked right now. But Kit has room at the table I squeezed him into."

"Kit's here?" Nik asked.

Philly nodded. "And he's got a girl with him. A client. He brought her here last night, too."

"I think your father was flirting with me," J.C. said as Nik hurried her down the stairs.

"He *was* flirting with you," Nik commented dryly.

"Ever since I can remember, he's flirted with all the girls that my brothers and I have brought to the restaurant."

"I suppose they were legion in numbers."

He shot her a look. "Not really. I'm a pretty quick learner. I stopped bringing my dates here sometime in high school."

"I like your family. Of course, I haven't met Theo yet. What's he like?"

"Classy," Nik said. "Don't tell me you didn't see his picture in the Sunday magazine section of the paper six months ago. He made the list of the ten most eligible bachelors in San Francisco."

"That was your brother Theo?"

He glanced down at her, a little annoyed at the stab of jealousy he felt at her tone. "Yeah. But it had its downside. There was a group of women who started appearing in his courtroom every time he had a case. His groupies. We razzed him about it until one of them turned into a stalker."

J.C.'s eyes widened. "Your brother had a stalker?"

Nik took her elbow when they reached the bottom of the stairs. "She followed him here one night and pulled a gun on him. Kit and I weren't here."

"What happened?"

"Theo talked her into going outside and he managed to get the gun away, but only after she shot him in the shoulder. Then he pressed charges."

"Good for him. He must have your father's charm to have talked her out of the gun."

Nik frowned at her. "You think my father's charming?"

"I think he's stunning. If he wants this Helena, he should just take her."

"That's not the way my dad operates. He's as conservative as they—"

A disturbance at the bar cut him off. They stared as Spiro picked a tall, beautiful older woman up off a bar stool and tossed her over his shoulder as if she were a featherweight. A moment later, he carried her through a door at the back of the bar. Applause broke out along with a few cheers and whistles.

"I assume that was Helena."

"What in the hell has gotten into my father?"

J.C. laughed. "I would say that Helena has."

Spotting his brother at a table close to the bar, Nik ran interference until they reached him. "Did I just see what I think I saw?"

Kit rose. "You did, and my friend here, Drew Merriweather, is the instigator. She encouraged Helena to buy a motorcycle."

"Helena bought a motorcycle?" Turning to J.C., he said, "Dad bought one three weeks ago."

"Your father, the conservative, bought a motorcycle?"

"We chalked it up to a continuation of his midlife crisis." Shaking his head, Nik grinned down at Kit's pretty friend. "Good job. It's high time one of them made a move. Drew, this is J.C. Riley."

As the two women exchanged greetings, Kit rose from his chair and offered it to J.C. "Enjoy, ladies. Nik and I have a little business to talk over."

"Well, that was rude," J.C. said as she sank into the chair across from Drew.

"He's not usually," Drew said as she offered J.C. half of her sandwich. "Kit, I mean."

"I figured you must be talking about Kit because Nik is rude all the time."

Drew blinked. "He is?"

"Yeah." She bit into the sandwich and studied the woman across from her. She was a pretty, petite blonde, and in spite of the fact that she looked totally put together in a simple sundress—something J.C. always aspired to and never quite achieved—Drew Merriweather looked as if she hadn't had any more sleep than J.C. Probably thanks to Kit, she mused.

Taking another bite of her sandwich, she spoke around it. "They're easy on the eyes though."

Drew shifted her gaze to Kit, then back again. "Yes."

The poor kid looked miserable, J.C. thought, and couldn't help but wonder if she looked a little bit like that herself. Men, she thought. Then she pushed the plate closer to Drew. "You've got to try this…" She paused to glance down at what she was holding. "What is it anyway?"

"A gyro," Drew said. "It's the specialty of the house. And Kit recommended the fries."

"Eat some," J.C. said. "You'll feel better. There's nothing like French fries or chocolate to lighten your mood."

NIK AND KIT kept their eyes on the TV screen over the bar as Nik punched the number of Rossi Investigations into his cell phone. When he was told that Cole was on another line, he said, "I'll hold."

Above them, Angelo Carlucci was still talking to TV

Five's star reporter, Carla Mitchell. Angelo had just informed all of San Francisco that Roman Oliver was the prime suspect in the killing of his son Paulo's bodyguard, and that he was sure Roman had also kidnapped Paulo.

Nik thoroughly agreed with his brother's summation of the situation. The shit had indeed hit the fan.

Carla Mitchell was milking the drama for all it was worth. She had dated Kit for a time, and when his brother had broken it off, she'd turned her attention to him.

It had only taken one date, a few drinks at a bar, for Nik to peg her as an ambitious woman who had her eye on a coanchor job on the evening news. And while he was all for ambition, he didn't want to be involved with a woman who was only interested in what inside police information he could provide to advance her career goals. Though they'd never discussed it, he assumed Kit had broken up with Carla for the same reason.

Nik had already filled Kit in on what he'd learned at the station that morning about the ransom notes being delivered to the two families and that there was an APB out on Sadie Oliver.

Kit had been the bearer of one piece of good news. The Oliver family had hired Theo to act as Roman's attorney. That was when Nik had decided to call Cole Buchanan at Rossi Investigations. The police would be under great pressure to move swiftly to close the case. The ten-million-dollar ransom was a powerful motivator. And so far, they seemed to be focusing all their attention on Roman Oliver and Sadie. That would only intensify as a result of Angelo Carlucci's interview.

So another suspect was needed—fast. Rossi Investigations could dig into the land deal the two families were competing over. No one in the city was better at following the money trail than they were. The way Nik figured it, the Rossi brothers could charge their usual fee to J.C.'s father.

"Detective Angelis," a voice spoke in his ear. "Mr. Buchanan will be tied up for a time. He'll get back to you."

After pocketing his cell phone, Nik brought up the subject Kit hadn't mentioned so far. And he figured that meant the news wasn't good. "How's Roman?"

Turning away from the TV screen, Kit glanced at his watch. "Last time I checked, he was still in surgery." He met Nik's eyes. "Even if the operation is successful and the swelling goes down, they might not know for a while if he'll be paralyzed."

"Yeah." Nik placed a hand on his brother's shoulder.

"Besides you and Theo, there's no one I'm closer to, and I feel so helpless."

"You're doing what you can to see that he doesn't get railroaded for murder and now this double kidnapping. And so am I."

"I don't feel like I'm making any progress on either score."

"Join the club." Nik nabbed a French fry off his brother's plate. "You know, J.C. says that it's like a recipe. Once we get all the ingredients, we'll know what happened. Rossi Investigations will dig up a few of those ingredients, and then we'll be cooking." Nik winced at his own pun and was surprised when Kit made no comment. He stole another French fry. "Actually, now that we know the bride and groom have been kidnapped, I think things are looking up for Roman. I could see him coming to the church, trying to stop the wedding and losing his temper. But this whole scenario of kidnapping his sister and holding her for ransom? There isn't a land deal in the world that would make Roman do that."

When his cell rang, he told Cole Buchanan what they needed, hung up and swiped another French fry. "How well do you know Sadie Oliver?"

Kit shook his head. "I only met her once very briefly, a year ago when her father got married. Both she and Juliana went to school in the east, and they were never at home when I visited the house. She's tall with dark hair, good-looking. She's twenty-six, four years younger than Roman and eight years older than Juliana. And she's smart. Roman is always saying that she's the brains in the family. She graduated from Harvard and blitzed through its law school in two years. Then she came home to join the family business."

"How's that going for her?"

He shrugged. "Roman says she's determined to run the company at his side one day. In her spare time, she volunteers to take pro bono cases from the public defender's office. She wants the trial experience. Why are you so interested in Sadie?"

"There's always the possibility that she acted alone."

Kit shot him a glare. "No way. How in hell did you come up with that ridiculous idea?"

Nik raised both hands, palms out. "Just trying to be objective." And it was clear to him that his brother wasn't. So he tried another tack. "If you don't like Sadie as the mastermind, how about Mario Oliver?"

"He's ruthless enough," Kit said. "But I don't think he would have botched it."

"If Roman wasn't in on it, maybe he interfered with his father's plan."

"Yeah, I can see that."

Nik took a sip of his beer. "What about this Michael Dano? What do you know about him?"

"He heads up the legal department. Roman has a lot of respect for him and depends on him a lot. I think he's hoping that Michael and Sadie will make a match of it."

"You said Sadie was smart. Could she be working with Dano? Could they have set this whole thing up together?"

Kit whirled and grabbed Nik by the lapels of his jacket. "You're saying she planned to kidnap her younger sister and frame her brother?"

"Easy," Nik said. "Somebody has to be objective enough to ask these questions."

"Right. You're right." Kit dropped his hands and leaned back against the bar. "Sorry. And the answer is yes, she's smart enough. But they're a close-knit family, as close as we are. Besides, if she or Roman were behind this, they wouldn't have made such a mess of it. And Sadie would never have run out on Roman. If she's missing, I think she's in trouble."

Nik took a swallow of beer. He'd thought about that possibility himself. He grabbed another fry and then frowned at his brother. This was the fourth time he'd swiped food, and Kit had yet to bat an eye. Probably because during the whole time they'd talked, Kit's eyes seldom had left his pretty blond friend.

Nik shifted his own gaze to J.C., who was deep in conversation with Drew. When she wasn't eating. She seemed to be enjoying Greek food with the same enthusiasm she brought to everything she did. He thought of the way she'd come into his office the night before and settled right into helping him think through the evidence they had so far. They might have been working together for years.

Watching her now as she laughed at something Drew said, he realized that he was letting his own fears turn him into a fool. It might be happening fast between them, but that didn't mean it wasn't right. They'd just have to make the time to see where things would lead between them. Bottom line, he was not going to let J.C. Riley walk out of his life.

Period. Even as he made the decision, his thumbs began to prick, and the fear that had settled rock-hard in his stomach melted. With a smile, he grabbed another French fry.

Once again, Kit didn't even notice. There was definitely something bothering his kid brother. Something besides Roman? This time when Nik shifted his gaze to the two women, he studied Drew more closely. She was small, she was blond and hadn't Philly said that Kit had been with her in the restaurant the night before?

"I just gave you a boatload of information, bro," Nik said. "Turnabout's fair play."

"What?" Kit asked.

"There's something you're not telling me and it has to do with Drew doesn't it?"

"No…I—"

"Dammit," he said as he turned on his brother. "She's part of it, isn't she? She's the mystery blonde, the woman that J.C. saw come into the church with Juliana."

11

J.C. WAVED A HAND in the direction of the bar. "They're about to get into a fight."

Drew glanced over and started to rise, but J.C. clamped a hand down on her arm. "Leave them be. I have four brothers, and they fight all the time. My stepmother boots them out of the house so that they don't break the furniture. Men. There's a basic genetic difference between them and us."

When Drew said nothing in reply, merely kept her gaze riveted on the two brothers, J.C. took another bite of the gyro, chewing thoughtfully. She had to figure out some kind of a game plan to handle Nik—and what she was beginning to feel for him. She glanced at the woman sitting across from her. If she didn't miss her guess, Drew was pretty much smitten with Kit. Luckily, she wasn't that far gone.

Yet.

The one little word had her setting down her gyro. Yet? It never worked out well to hide from the truth. If she wasn't already, she was certainly in danger of being smitten with Nik Angelis. She pressed a hand over her heart when she felt the little flutter. Maybe Nik was doing her a favor by backing off and returning their status to sex buddies. She certainly wasn't ready to take that headlong plunge into love. Love? No. Smitten was one thing. Love was a different ball of wax entirely. She had to think about this.

Sometimes it helped her if she talked out loud. "Of course, there's the physical difference, too. I can handle that difference. In fact, I enjoy handling it." Great sex. That's what she had with Nik. The best sex she'd ever had in her life. She definitely didn't want that to end—yet.

When she realized that she once more had Drew's attention, J.C. smiled at her, then jerked her head in the direction of Nik and Kit. "They certainly are magnificent specimens, aren't they?"

"They're beautiful. The first time I saw Kit, he reminded me of a fallen angel."

"Good description. The first time I saw Nik I thought of Adonis, the mortal man who had two goddesses fighting over him."

"They're certainly something to fight over."

Or *for,* J.C. thought. Drew had shifted her gaze to Kit again. J.C. purposely kept her eyes on the food. Looking at Nik didn't help her think, and she needed every single one of her brain cells. She picked up a French fry and squeezed lemon on it the way she'd seen Drew just do.

Truth told, whatever her feelings for Nik were, she'd be more than willing to fight for him. So what they had right now was great sex. Maybe the whole key was to approach the situation the way a man did. For them good sex was often enough. Perhaps that's what Nik had been trying to tell her all morning. And that was fine. Wasn't it?

Pushing the question away, she concentrated on the food. "You should have some of this gyro. It's excellent. I really have to get the recipe."

"But Kit is not an angel," Drew said suddenly.

J.C. met her eyes. "Neither is Nik."

"Kit's a stubborn, determined man. He pretends to listen, and then he just goes and does exactly what he wants."

J.C. leaned forward. "I'd say it runs in the family because you could be talking about Nik." Then she grinned. "They must get it from their dad. Looked like he was about to get his way when we walked in."

"It's not fair. And I can't let him make every decision for me. I think…I'm afraid I'm the kind of woman who does that—leans on a man, I mean."

J.C. lifted the wineglass and handed it to her. "You're afraid of that? Don't you know?"

Drew shook her head. "I can't remember anything about myself. I have amnesia."

J.C. almost spat out a mouthful of gyro. "Amnesia? Seriously? I can't imagine." She might have problems with her family, but she didn't want to think what it would be like to not remember them. "Did you want to talk about it?"

Drew did, everything from the moment she walked into Kit's office and hired him until they'd come to the restaurant for lunch.

When she was finished, J.C. said, "So you're the mystery woman, the one I saw get out of the car with the bride."

"I guess. I can't remember anything. I just get flashes now and then."

J.C. squeezed her hand. "You'll remember."

Drew leaned closer to J.C. "I have to turn myself in. People are following Kit because of me, and he could probably lose his license for not turning me in to the police."

"You're sloppy in love with him, aren't you?"

"No. Of course, not." Drew glanced at J.C. and took a long swallow of wine. "And I'm not going to fall in love with him. He's…we're…that's not going to happen. It can't."

She looked at Kit again and then back at J.C. "I'm going to need your help. All you have to do is keep Kit distracted for a few minutes. Tell him I've gone to the ladies' room. Can you do that? Please?"

"If that's what you want." She gave Drew two thumbs up. "We women have to stick together, don't we?"

As Drew rose from the table, J.C. beamed a smile at Kit and mouthed, "Ladies' room." Then, because she didn't want her gaze to stray to Nik, she returned her attention to the plate of food in front of her. She lifted the gyro, then set it back on the plate. It was delicious. She just wasn't hungry, and she knew why.

She'd seen her possible future in Drew's eyes. She'd seen what it was like to be in love—the misery, the uncertainty, the fear. Wasn't it lucky she'd decided that all she wanted was to be sex buddies with Nik? She pushed the plate of food away.

"DON'T TELL ME you're not hungry," Nik said as he sat down in the chair that Drew had just vacated.

"Okay." J.C. folded her arms on the table and lifted her chin. "I won't tell you I'm not hungry."

The combative look in her eyes told Nik that he hadn't found the right approach. But that seemed to be his modus operandi where J.C. was concerned. He set his glass of beer down, then suddenly frowned. "Don't you like Greek food? If you don't like gyros, there are other things on the menu that you'd love." He signaled the waitress.

"I love Greek food. The gyro was delicious. I'm going to talk your father into giving me the recipe for the sauce he uses. It's amazing. I'm just full."

Nik studied her as she grabbed the wineglass and drained it. "Something's wrong."

"No. We should get back to the police station."

He put a hand on her arm to keep her in her chair. "We will." He'd figured out what was bothering her while he'd been talking to his brother. She was a woman and they'd just spent the night together. She needed to talk about it, sort it out. Women always needed to talk. So they'd talk.

"What can I get you?"

"Hi, Mandy." Nik beamed a smile at the waitress. "I'll have coffee."

"I'll have more wine," J.C. said.

"Make that two coffees," Nik amended. "And forget the wine."

"No," J.C. began, but Mandy had already hurried away. She glared at Nik. "I wanted more wine."

"You don't need more wine. I need you to work with a sketch artist when we get back to the station, and I don't want you seeing double."

She met his gaze squarely. "You don't need more coffee. You drank about a gallon of it this morning. It isn't good for you."

He smiled at her. "Relax. The stuff they serve up at the station isn't coffee. It's some kind of brown colored sludge."

"You're a bully."

He cocked an eyebrow at her. "And you're not."

"Only in self-defense. I have four brothers."

His smile widened. "I have two."

"But you're the oldest."

"Touché." Nik had the pleasure of seeing her lips twitch, but she tried to hide it by taking a drink of water. He was almost getting used to the flutter of panic in his stomach every time he looked at her. But he wanted to put a stop to it. His brother was tied up in knots over Drew Merriweather. He didn't intend for that to happen to him. He was going to talk to J.C. about their relationship and lay it out for her. Get it settled. But he'd interviewed enough perps and witnesses to know the value of an indirect approach. "Did Drew tell you that she's the mystery blonde?"

Her eyes flew to his. "Don't you *dare* arrest her. She has amnesia. And she's going to turn herself in."

"I'm not going to arrest her. Kit is sure she's not involved in the kidnapping, and he asked for some time. He thinks she's close to recovering her memory, and he's promised to bring her to the station as soon as she does. So I don't think that he's going to let her turn herself in just yet."

J.C.'s chin lifted. "A girl's got to do what a girl's got to do."

"So does a man." Over J.C.'s shoulder, Nik watched Kit enter the ladies' room. He had a pretty good idea of just what his brother was thinking of doing, and he had to suppress a grin as he shifted his gaze back to J.C. He had her attention now, so he should go ahead and tell her what he'd decided.

Mandy set coffee in front of them, and he took a sip of his. "Were you telling Philly the truth? Is your dream to run a restaurant like this?"

She glanced up in surprise. "Yes. Not this big, of course. My plan was to start with the catering, build up a reputation, and then open a small place." She glanced around. "I'd like it to have this kind of a welcoming feel."

"And it all started when you walked into the American Culinary Institute?"

She sipped her coffee. "Just by chance."

"Or by fate," Nik said. "My aunt Cass believes that the Fates are always offering choices. It's up to the person to make the right one, and it looks like you did."

"Maybe," she said.

Nik studied her as she sipped her coffee. He'd never before put too much stock in his aunt Cass's talk about the Fates. But he was beginning to wonder...

A small cheer went up at the bar just then, and Nik and J.C. glanced over to see Spiro and Helena step hand in hand through the doorway that led from the kitchen. They were smiling, and when Spiro drew Helena close and kissed her, there was another cheer.

"Looks like they settled some things between them," J.C. said with a grin. "Helena seems to have put a stop to the caveman tactics."

Looking at his father's face, Nik had a pretty good idea of just how they'd settled things. About time, he thought. Though he couldn't help but wonder just what space they'd chosen to do their "settling" in. For a second, he shifted his gaze to the ladies' room that Kit and Drew had yet to exit from. He figured they were settling things, too.

"I'll bet they made love," J.C. said.

"I was thinking the same thing myself." Then his eyes widened as Spiro and Helena stepped out from behind the bar and began to thread their way through the crowd and up the stairs. They stopped only to exchange a few words with Philly before they disappeared. "I don't believe it."

"Why not? Your father's a very attractive man, and Helena's a beautiful woman. And you said—"

Nik lost track of what J.C. was saying for a minute as his sister flashed him a grin and a thumbs-up sign.

"I don't see why you'd be surprised that your father and Helena would want to express their feelings in a physical way."

Nik shifted his gaze back to J.C. "I'm not at all surprised that my father and Helena very probably just made love in Helena's office." Although he knew from experience that wasn't the only place they could have used. "What I find hard to believe is that it's the middle of the lunch hour rush, and they're both leaving. That never happens. The one thing that they've always seemed to have in common is they're workaholics when it comes to the restaurant."

J.C. grinned at him. "I'll bet they're going to take a ride on their motorcycles. It's a great day for it. I envy them."

Nik did, too, and he felt a little band of pain tighten in his chest as J.C.'s grin began to fade. He knew exactly what she was thinking because he was right on the same page. Reaching out, he took her hand and raised it to his lips. "I wish that we could just play hooky, too. I'm giving you a rain check. When this is all over, when you're safe, we'll borrow those bikes and I'll take you to my grandfather's fishing cabin. Then I'll take you sailing on *Athena.*"

He wanted to see her there, Nik realized, in the cabin, on his sailboat. More than that, he wanted to be with her there. And he wanted to find a way to tell her that. Something cold and hard settled in his stomach. Fear? No way. His father had settled things with Helena. Kit was settling things with Drew. And he was going to settle things with J.C.

Leaning forward, he said, "I think we should clear up what's going on between us."

J.C. met his eyes. He would have thought her to be perfectly calm, but she was clasping her hands together on the table and her knuckles had gone white. "I think what's going on between us is perfectly clear. We're buddies."

Nik studied her. "You still feel that way after last night."

She returned his gaze steadily. But her knuckles turned even whiter. "We agreed from the beginning that our relationship was going to be friendly and sexual. No demands. After all, we're both in careers where we have obligations twenty-four-seven. Neither of us has the time for a more serious relationship."

That was true. Hadn't he used the same line of reasoning on the women he'd dated when they'd shown signs of wanting more? Why was it making him furious to hear *her* say it?

"I like the sex. Very much."

"Yeah," he managed, when what he wanted to do

was to shake her. But he had enough fisherman's blood in him to know that sometimes you had to give your catch some line if you wanted to reel it in.

"Okay. I'm glad we cleared that up." He tried a smile. "Sex buddies it is." For *now*, he added to himself. Because he couldn't stop himself, he grasped her chin. "But one thing you ought to know. I don't do one-night stands. We're going to continue to be sex buddies even after we get Snake Eyes. Understood?"

"Sure."

"Let's go back to the station." As they rose and he guided her out of The Poseidon, Nik made a vow. He'd play along with her for now, but Ms. J.C. Riley was going to learn that he wasn't going to be satisfied with half a loaf for long.

12

J.C. FOLDED HER HANDS on the top of Nik's desk and gazed around his office. It was a small room, not much larger than the one he used as his work space in his apartment. And it was just as sparsely furnished. There was a desk, two filing cabinets, a small computer table holding a flat screen and a keyboard, and two straight-backed chairs.

Through the half-slanted blinds, she had a view of the squad room. It was bustling, and even through the closed door, she could hear the sounds of phones ringing and voices talking. Burnt coffee scented the air.

She spotted Nik standing in the doorway of what he'd said was an observation room. He'd gone to talk to Kit. She saw two other men enter the squad room. They'd drawn her eye because the taller of the two had to be the third Angelis brother, Theo. He had the same dark hair and drop-dead good looks as his brothers, but unlike Kit and Nik, who favored jeans and sport coats, this man evidently liked Italian suits. And he wore them very well.

Moving with a slow, languid grace, Theo escorted the younger man with him to one of the desks, then turned and strolled toward Nik. He was taller, and while

Nik had a definite air of ruggedness about him, Theo seemed to radiate a sort of elegant maleness. He was just the kind of urban sophisticate that her stepmother was always introducing her to. She watched as he followed Nik into the observation room. She'd seen Captain Parker escort Drew into an adjoining room, where she assumed he was questioning her.

Kit and Drew had had a busy afternoon. Nik had filled her in on most of it while she'd been working with the sketch artist. Drew had gotten her memory back. She had designed Juliana Oliver's wedding dress, and at the last minute, Juliana had invited her to be maid of honor at the wedding. Drew had also shot one of the bad guys, the same one she claimed had fought with Roman Oliver and pushed him down the stairs. Then this afternoon, she and Kit had managed to trap two of the shooters from the church, the one Drew had shot and his sidekick, and they were now in custody. Nik had arranged for J.C. to take a look at them, but neither of them was the man who'd shot Father Mike.

The young police artist had just completed the sketch of Snake Eyes to her satisfaction. A copy of it lay on the desk in front of her, but she'd turned it facedown. Looking at it made her stomach queasy.

Nik had told her that they'd scan it and run it through a program that just might give them a match. In J.C.'s opinion, they were due for a little luck. Turning her attention back to the room, she opened a drawer and found a neat stack of small notebooks, the size that would easily fit into a pocket. Cop-sized, she supposed. Beside them lay two boxes—one with sharpened pencils and the other with inexpensive ballpoint pens. A quick search through the other drawers revealed neatly labeled files, tissues, extra handcuffs.

The man was almost obsessively neat and organized. And he didn't have so much as a crumb of food stashed away. How could he work without it? She let her gaze return to the box of chocolates that sat in the far corner of the desk. Every time she looked at them, her heart did a little flutter.

Nik had given them to her as a reward when the sketch was finished. She ran a finger over the bow. The chocolates were from Ghirardelli's. He must have sent someone out to get them. For her.

It was so sweet of him. And romantic. J.C. folded her hands together on the desk. There was no more avoiding it. The sketch was finished, she'd conducted her little snoop-a-thon, and now she had to think about what the gift might mean.

He'd given her chocolates. And not just any chocolates. The ones she'd nagged him about earlier in the day. Nik Angelis didn't seem like the kind of guy who would do something that sweet. Unable to help herself, she reached out and fingered the bow again.

When she and Nik had been sitting there in The Poseidon, he'd wanted to clear things up between them. But could she let him talk first? No. Of course not.

J.C. dropped her head into her hands. When was she going to learn to keep her mouth shut? Once she got on a roll, she couldn't seem to turn it off. And now she was paying the piper. With her big mouth she'd convinced Nik that they ought to remain sex buddies. She'd read something in his eyes that had suggested he might want something more, but she'd cut him off and jabbered right over him. Blah, blah, blah, blah, blah!

So instead, they were going to be what? Long-term sex buddies? And she had only herself to blame for the whole situation. She'd been the one who'd suggested it—just another example of how she led with her mouth. First chance she got, she was going to burn that copy of *Cosmo!*

Drawing the box of chocolates closer, she pulled off the ribbon. She selected the most decadent-looking confection, popped it into her mouth and chewed. Across the squad room, Captain Parker came out of an interrogation room and went into the observation room where Nik and Kit were.

Then J.C. suddenly frowned down at the box of chocolates. The piece she'd just eaten had looked better than it had tasted. A whole lot better. Her frown deepened. In fact, the flavor had reminded her a bit of sawdust.

She closed the box and pushed it away. This was simply not going to happen. Nik Angelis was not going to spoil the taste of chocolate for her. Somehow, she was going to have to figure a way to convince him that he wanted more than no-strings sex with her.

When she glanced into the squad room again, she saw Theo exiting with the tall, young man he'd entered with. Then Kit came out of a room with his arm around Drew and led her toward the door. She would have bet the box of Ghirardelli's that buddy sex was not on Kit and Drew's agenda tonight.

Still frowning, she watched Nik and Captain Parker enter an office across the squad room from where she sat. She was rising, intending to go to them, when she froze. Another couple had entered the squad room just as Kit and Drew left. The woman had every male eye in the room locking on her. She was young and beautiful—a tall blonde with eyes nearly the color of the huge sapphire ring she had on her hand. She was wearing a peach-colored suit that showcased a perfectly shaped hourglass figure. The jacket barely kept her ample breasts holstered. And those stiletto heels that drew attention to long, slender legs must have had most of the men in the squad room going cross-eyed, trying to decide which asset to focus on.

But it wasn't the blond beauty that had J.C. frozen in her chair. It was the man on her arm.

Turning over the sketch on Nik's desk, she glanced at it and then back at the man. His hair was different. On Friday night it had been slicked back close to his head. Today it fell in loose dark waves nearly to his shoulders. His clothes were different, too. The man who'd shot Father Mike had worn black jeans and a black long-sleeved T-shirt. In short, he'd looked like a thug. The man on the well-packaged blonde's arm looked like an expensive gigolo. He wore a snakeskin jacket, ivory trousers and a pale yellow shirt, open at the throat and showcasing a thick gold chain. But the diamond on his pinky was the same ring Snake Eyes had worn. She was sure of it.

The man glanced in her direction, and as he met her gaze, any lingering doubt in her mind vanished. She was looking at the man who wanted to kill her.

NIK FOLLOWED D.C. Parker into his office and shut the door. "Thanks for going easy on my brother, Captain."

Parker sent him an amused glance. "Did you think

I was going to charge him after he saved the SFPD some money by bringing in two of the shooters?"

"You might have. He harbored a material witness."

"Who wouldn't have been much use to us as long as she had amnesia. You want to be captain someday, right, Angelis?"

"Yeah."

"Pretend he's not your brother, and tell me what would you have done in my shoes?"

Nik grinned. "I would have let him walk out that door."

There was a sudden hush in the normal din in the squad room. For a count of three beats the only sound in the area was the ring of a few phones. He and Parker looked out through the glass windows.

A couple stood in the doorway. *Rich* and *flashy* were the two words that popped into Nik's mind. But it was the woman that had every cop in the room staring. The blonde radiated moneyed sex. The man on her arm had a little less polish, but Nik would bet he'd spent more time on his hairstyle than she had.

He spoke in a low tone to his captain. "Who the hell are—"

D.C. Parker moved toward the door of his office. "Mr. and Mrs. Frankie Carlucci. I invited them here. I'm expecting someone from the Oliver family in a little while. I've offered to keep them personally updated on the case. Commissioner Galvin wants me to ooze understanding and cooperation in an attempt to keep the tension between the two families at a minimum. C'mon, I'll introduce you—give you a taste of what it's like to walk around in a captain's shoes."

As they moved through the squad room, Nik recalled

that Frankie was Angelo Carlucci's much younger step-brother. Nik guessed his age to be in his mid to late thirties, and the woman on his arm looked to be in her early twenties.

"Mr. and Mrs. Carlucci," Parker said as he extended his hand, "I want you to meet Detective Nik Angelis. He's the man who arrived first on the scene at St. Peter's last night."

"A pleasure," Frankie said.

"Please call me Gina. Mrs. Carlucci sounds so formal." The blonde spoke in a breathy voice that Nik suspected was meant to remind him of Marilyn Monroe.

"It's a pleasure, Gina." Nik shook her hand. Then he grasped Frankie's. His thumbs were pricking when he pulled them away. He studied the man more carefully.

"You look as though you've recovered far more quickly than I have from the charity ball at the St. Regis last night," Parker said to Gina Carlucci.

"I don't see how," Gina said. "We haven't slept since we got the news about poor Paulo. It's horrible. Angelo is devastated."

"Tell me you've arrested Roman Oliver," Frankie added. "We know that he was there. He obviously came to stop the wedding."

"We're working on the case," Parker replied.

"Yes. Of course you are. But my brother Angelo isn't as young as he used to be, and Paulo is his only son, the apple of his eye. He's going to want justice, and soon."

"No. Stop." Dodging desks and sidestepping cops, J.C. raced as fast as she could across the squad room.

"He's the one." It had been the sight of Nik shaking Snake Eyes's hand that had finally melted her paralysis.

She skidded to a stop and pointed. "Arrest him. He's the one who shot Father Mike!"

"Shot Father Mike?" Eyebrows raised, the man turned to Parker. "What is she talking about?"

"I'm talking about shooting a priest on the altar of St. Peter's Church last night," J.C. said. "Don't tell me you have short-term memory loss? I saw you."

"Ms. Riley…" Captain Parker began.

"Good heavens, *who* is this?" the blonde breathed.

Ignoring the blonde, J.C. continued, "You would have killed him if I hadn't hit you with my cell phone."

Snake Eyes turned to D.C. Parker and spoke in a calm voice. "Is this what you invited us down here for, Captain? To be accosted and falsely accused like this? Perhaps, I should have brought my lawyer."

"No, that won't be—" Parker began again.

"I think it might be a very good idea." J.C. moved until she was standing toe-to-toe with Frankie. "You tried to kill me, too."

"J.C." Nik inserted himself between J.C. and the man she was accusing, easing her back a little.

"Check the back of his head. I bet there's a mark where I hit him." She raised the sketch and waved it. "And look at this! He's the man I saw."

"Let me see that." Frankie took the sketch out of her hand. After glancing at it briefly, he smiled and passed it to his wife. "I'm afraid that this doesn't do me justice, darling."

"Hardly." Gina gave a breathy laugh as she gave it to Parker.

Nik's grip on her arms tightened, preventing her from launching herself at Frankie Carlucci.

"He's Snake Eyes!"

"Detective Angelis, will you please take Ms. Riley into my office?" Parker asked.

J.C. whirled on Parker. "You're not going to arrest him?"

"I'm afraid not," Parker said. "You see, I can provide Mr. and Mrs. Carlucci with an alibi from six p.m. on Friday up until the time I received the call from Detective Angelis. So can Commissioner Galvin and hundreds of other people who were attending the charity ball at the St. Regis that night, including your stepmother."

13

THE MOMENT NIK CLOSED the door to Parker's office, J.C. twisted out of his grip, whirled and gave him a hard shove. "You don't believe me."

Grabbing her hands, Nik growled, "Calm down. I do believe you. Hell, my thumbs started pricking the moment I shook his hands."

"Really?"

"Yes. But we need to think about this."

"Think? What is there to think about? And who is he that he's so chummy with your captain?"

"Sit." He shoved her into a chair, then moved to slant the blinds and block them from the curious gazes in the squad room. "I don't want to put on more of a show than we already have."

"It wasn't a show. I'm telling you—"

"Just shut up a minute." Kneeling down in front of her, he grabbed her hands. "First, the man you're accusing is Frankie Carlucci, youngest brother of Angelo, who runs the Carlucci business interests."

"Snake Eyes is the bridegroom's uncle?"

"Yeah."

"Then he might have had just as great a motive as Roman Oliver to stop that wedding."

"That's exactly what I'm thinking. Except he has an ironclad alibi, and Roman doesn't."

"Any chance he has a twin brother?" she asked.

"No. And right now his alibi isn't my main concern."

"Why not?"

"Let's go with what we both believe—that in spite of the fact that Captain Parker is giving him an alibi, Frankie Carlucci is your Snake Eyes. You with me so far?"

She nodded.

"Good. The man has the balls to walk right in here. He knows you saw him without his mask. He must have suspected that there'd be an artist's sketch of him by this time. So he gussies himself up until he looks like he's ready to pose for the cover of a pricey man's fashion magazine. He's confident about his alibi. After all, Parker will be here to back him up. But it's still risky. And there's a chance that you'll be here and cause a scene."

"A lot of good it did," J.C. said.

"Oh, I'm thinking it did some good all right. Just not for you."

"What do you mean?"

"He volunteers to come here representing his family, and he not only establishes that he couldn't be the man you saw at the church, but he also knows exactly where you are now, and if he's smart enough to make some basic deductions, he knows that I'm probably assigned to protect you."

Her hands tightened on his. "You think he'll try to kill me again."

"Jude Catherine, I'll promise you one thing. I'm not going to give him the chance."

THE TENSION in Captain Parker's office was so thick that J.C. would have had to use one of her Japanese Santoku knives to hack through it. D.C. Parker was standing with his hands in his pockets, staring out his window. Nik was pacing behind her chair, anger radiating off of him in waves. The bone of contention was the sketch that the police artist had drawn. It was lying on Parker's desk, and even J.C. had to admit that it wasn't a mirror likeness of Frankie Carlucci.

Nik might believe that Frankie Carlucci was the man who'd shot Father Mike, but his captain wasn't convinced.

"Look," she said, "I understand that he looked a lot different when he walked in here this afternoon. But last night he was wearing a ski mask and he'd tied his hair back into a ponytail. That's the way I described him for the sketch. Today, he looked as if he'd just stepped out of a hair salon."

"He probably did just step out of a hair salon," Nik muttered behind her.

Parker turned from the window. "I understand what you're saying, Ms. Riley, but the fact remains that eyewitness testimony does not have a high rate of accuracy. Based on the statistics alone, you may very well be mistaken."

"She's not," Nik said.

Parker ignored him.

J.C. couldn't have put into words what it meant to her that Nik believed her, but she didn't want him to get in trouble with his captain. Still, she knew Frankie Carlucci was the man. "I'm not mistaken."

Parker looked directly at her when he spoke. "Even

if I do believe you, there's the matter of his alibi. Many people, including your stepmother and your father, can testify that he was in the grand ballroom at the St. Regis Hotel during the time that Father Mike was shot. Your stepmother cochaired that event with Gina Carlucci."

"You had your eyes on him every single minute?" Nik asked.

"It was hard not to. The ballroom had a balcony with tables set up along the railing. Frankie and Gina Carlucci were seated at one of those tables. They were in plain sight up until the time that I got your call from the church and left."

Nik paused to place his hands on J.C.'s shoulders. "He's the one, Captain. Maybe you're too focused on charging Roman Oliver to see that."

The tension in the office grew even thicker. When Captain Parker finally spoke, his voice was low but clipped. "I'm going to forget you said that, Detective Angelis. And I'm going to point out to you that your own view of this case might be suffering from a bit of tunnel vision as well. I know that Roman Oliver has been a good friend to your family. Perhaps you're so focused on finding evidence that proves what you want to prove that you're blind to the facts."

"One of the *facts* is that Drew Merriweather claims that Roman was trying to help the bride and groom," Nik argued.

"Or he was pretending to," Parker said. "He may have been putting on a show for his sister."

"A show that included having one of the shooters shoving him down the stairs?" Nik asked.

"Accidents happen."

"With all due respect, sir—"

"Not another word, Angelis." With a sigh, Parker sat down at his desk. "You're not working this case. You're assigned to protect Ms. Riley. But I'm going to tell you about the latest report that I received from the lab. Roman and Sadie Oliver left prints on both of the ransom notes that were sent out to the families."

Her stomach sinking, J.C. placed her hand over Nik's.

"That's impossible," Nik said.

"No. That's hard evidence," Parker replied. "And based on it, I'm going to arrest Roman Oliver just as soon as the doctors say he can have visitors."

A knock on the door interrupted them. "Come in."

Theo Angelis opened the door, then stopped. "Sorry. I can come back if this isn't a good time."

J.C. twisted in her chair to see Theo and the young man who'd left with him earlier.

"Nik," Theo said, nodding at his brother. "I hope I'm not interrupting."

"Not at all. This is as good a time as any," Parker said. "Since your brother will no doubt pass everything along that I say to him, I might as well save the two of you some time." He gestured toward J.C. "This is Ms. J.C. Riley. She saw the man who shot Father Mike, and your brother has been assigned to protect her. She's just identified him as Frankie Carlucci, but I've given Frankie an ironclad alibi. As Roman Oliver's counsel, you'll do your best to break it, but I'll warn you that hundreds of others, including Commissioner Galvin and Ms. Riley's stepmother, will confirm my testimony."

"I see." Theo nodded at J.C. and then returned his

gaze to Parker and nodded in the direction of the young man next to him. "I've brought my intern along. This is Sam Schaeffer. He's finishing his last year at Stanford. I hope you don't mind if he takes notes."

"Not at all," Parker said.

Theo's intern could be worth a second glance, too, J.C. decided, if he'd stop slouching and look up from the floor. He was younger, perhaps in his early twenties and was built along more slender lines than the Angelis brothers. He wore his dark hair a bit longish, and though he'd slicked it back, a few stray locks had tumbled forward onto his forehead.

"Is there any other bad news you want to pass on to me?" Theo asked.

"Sure." Parker sent him a grim smile. "I was just telling your brother that we have enough evidence to arrest Roman Oliver. His fingerprints and those of his sister Sadie were found on both of the ransom notes."

Sam Schaeffer dropped the notebook he was carrying. As he stooped to retrieve it, he asked, "Is Mr. Oliver that stupid that he would leave prints on the ransom notes?"

"Even the smartest criminals make mistakes," Theo said. "But based on my personal knowledge of Mr. Oliver, I would say he isn't that stupid."

"At last, the voice of reason," Nik murmured.

"I tend to agree," Parker said. "Otherwise I would not be sharing information so freely with Roman Oliver's defense counsel."

For a moment, there was dead silence in the room, and J.C. felt the strain between Nik and his captain ease for the first time. Oddly enough, the tension in the room now seemed to be emanating from Sam Schaeffer. The young man's knuckles were white where he was gripping his pen.

"Having said that," D.C. Parker continued, "I'm obliged to act on the evidence. Roman Oliver came to the church, we believe he fought with Paulo Carlucci, and we know that he shot and killed Gino DeLucca, Paulo's bodyguard. Sadie Oliver was also at the church, as indicated by her purse, so she could very well be Roman's accomplice. Given the high-profile nature of the case and the fact that all of this will eventually be leaked to the press, I believe that we have no choice other than to arrest Roman Oliver."

J.C. felt Nik's grip tighten on her shoulders.

When Parker's phone rang, Theo moved closer to Nik and spoke in a low voice. "My friend in the D.A.'s office has been reporting to me on the progress of the investigation. I'm pretty sure they won't arrest him today because the doctors are keeping Roman sedated."

"Kit just left for the hospital. What's Roman's prognosis?" Nik asked.

"His father says the doctors were able to relieve the swelling on the base of his spinal cord, and they're very hopeful. They'll know more tomorrow."

"He didn't do this, Theo," Nik said.

"And we're going to prove that."

J.C. saw a look pass between the two brothers. Theo's slow way of talking, his matter-of-fact tone and easy manner, was calming Nik. She felt his hands relax a bit and some of her own tension eased. The only person in the room now who seemed to be wound up tight was Sam Schaeffer.

NIK STUDIED his brother. "You think it's a frame?"

Theo glanced at Parker and then returned his gaze to Nik. "A damn good one."

"Do you have any other leads?"

"I'm working on some. What about you?"

"I have Rossi Investigations trying to track down how this whole thing is related to that big land deal. It has to be. And alibi or not, Frankie Carlucci is involved and he may not have acted on his own."

"Maybe not," Theo said. "In the meantime, everything is being leaked to the press. Carla Mitchell has already broadcast news about the ransom notes on Channel Five."

Nik frowned. "How did that leak out?"

Theo's lips curved slightly. "The Feds are handling that piece of the case. You'll have to ask them. But the same thing will happen here. Both Angelo Carlucci and Mario Oliver will be pushing Commissioner Galvin for information. There were news cameras outside when Sam and I came in. We only avoided them because Frankie and Gina Carlucci were offering an interview."

"Dammit," Nik muttered. "That lowlife *is* the man J.C. saw shoot Father Mike on the altar."

Theo shifted his gaze to J.C. "You're sure."

"I know he's the one," J.C. said.

"Frankie Carlucci isn't the brightest light in the Carlucci family," Theo said. "He's even earned the nickname 'Fredo,' based on one of Don Corleone's sons in *The Godfather*—the one who was a bit of a bungler."

"You've done your homework," Nik commented.

"My intern is good at research."

"Yeah, well if we're going to use movie analogies, what about *Fargo?*" J.C. asked. "The killers in that movie were bunglers of the highest order, but they left quite a few bodies in their wake."

Sam laughed suddenly. "She's right."

"Thanks," J.C. said.

"But for the time being, our boy Frankie has an alibi," Nik pointed out. He flicked a glance at his captain. Since Parker had picked up the call, he hadn't said more than two or three words. Nik had a feeling that more bad news was coming.

"Keep me posted on what you learn from the Rossis," Theo instructed.

Nik shifted his gaze to Sam Schaeffer, who was talking to J.C. "Since when do you work with an intern, bro?"

"I was lucky enough to get Sam this morning. I figure since time is of the essence here, I can use the extra help."

"Ms. Riley." D.C. Parker hung up the phone. "That was your father. He wanted to remind you of the garden party brunch your stepmother is throwing tomorrow. He expects you to be there at noon."

"Forget it. It's too dangerous," Nik said.

"Mayor Riley anticipated your reaction, Detective Angelis, and he said to tell you that two agents from Rossi Investigations will be there to provide all the assistance you need. He said you knew them—Cole Buchanan and Pepper Rossi? If you don't think that will be sufficient, Commissioner Galvin and I will also be in attendance."

"I'm supposed to put in an appearance myself," Theo said.

"Do I have anything to say about this?" J.C. rose from her chair.

"Yes," Nik said. "I think that the choice should be left to J.C."

"Your father said that he expects you to be there," Parker stated. "Was he correct?"

She hesitated for only one beat before she said, "Yes."

"What?" Nik asked. He'd been sure that she'd refuse. "You can't be serious."

J.C. met his eyes. "I have to go. It's an election year."

"J.C.—"

"Now that we've settled that," Parker said, "this is what I'm going to suggest to *you*, Detective Angelis. I suggest that you focus your attention totally on protecting Ms. Riley. Are you following me?"

"Yes, sir." Nik nodded.

"Since the man who shot Father Mike is still at large, I'm ordering you to forget about investigating this case and do the job you've been assigned."

Nik felt the knot in his stomach grow tighter. What Parker was saying was crystal clear to him. The bottom line was that Frankie Carlucci wasn't going to be arrested anytime soon, so he was free to take shots at J.C. whenever he pleased.

"I have to go with the evidence, but that doesn't mean that the case is closed," Parker said. "Or that I'm not looking objectively at other options. So focus on your job, and let me do mine."

"Yes, sir," Nik replied.

"That's all, Detective."

14

"YOU'RE ANGRY with me," J.C. said as they stepped out of the station.

"I'm not."

"Then what is it?"

"I've just got a bad feeling."

"Your thumbs again?"

"Shit!"

"What?" J.C. glanced around, but all she saw was a reporter from Channel Five news racing toward them.

"Nik." The woman beamed a smile as she stepped into his path. "Be a dear and give me something. I couldn't get anything from Kit."

"You've been getting more than you should be getting, Carla."

She tossed back her hair and laughed. "What can I say? I'm good at my job."

"I don't have anything."

"C'mon. You were first on the scene at the church. For old time's sake."

"No comment." Grabbing J.C.'s hand, Nik made a move to get around her, but Carla countered it, and her cameraman joined them.

"Frankie Carlucci says the police have enough evidence to arrest Roman Oliver for murder and kidnapping, but they're dragging their feet. I'm giving you equal time."

"No comment." This time Nik made it past her.

Carla did a little double step to keep up. "It's your case. Give me a crumb, or I'll have to go with Frankie's accusation."

"It's not—" J.C. began, then shut up when Nik tightened his grip on her hand.

Carla shifted her smile to J.C. "I recognize you. You're Mayor Riley's daughter, aren't you? What is your involvement in the case, Ms. Riley?"

Nik edged J.C. toward the corner. "Ms. Riley is not involved in the case. We're dating. I'm taking her to dinner. And you can quote me on that."

The words had come out on a snarl. Nik was definitely angry at *someone*. As soon as they'd crossed the street and they were out of the reporter's earshot, J.C. said, "It's my father's garden party, right? That's what you're so angry about. I'm sorry, but I have to go to it."

"I get it," Nik muttered. "You think your father needs you. I'd do the same thing in your shoes. It's your father I'd like to strangle. I'm going to have a little talk with him."

"Oh." Her mind filled with the image of Nik going toe-to-toe with her father. "Maybe not—"

"Hurry!"

"My legs are shorter than yours." She was running to keep up by the time they reached the corner. "Why the rush? And why are we going in this direction? The parking lot is back that way."

"I'm doing exactly what Parker told me to do," Nik said, urging her across the intersection with the rest of the pedestrians. "Making sure that you're safe. I'm not taking the chance that Frankie Carlucci knows my car by now. And I'm not taking a chance that he might have someone waiting for us in that garage. If you'd like a movie analogy, think of the exploding cars in *The Pelican Brief.*"

Swallowing hard, she glanced over her shoulder. "He wouldn't try something right outside the police station, would he?"

"He tried something right outside of St. Peter's Church. You made a good point to Theo. The fact that Frankie's not very smart doesn't mean that he can't be deadly."

A little wave of panic rolled through her, and she didn't object when Nik broke into a run. "You're scaring me."

"I'm scaring myself."

At the next corner, he pushed her into a fancy coffee shop.

"We're stopping for coffee?"

"We're stopping so that I can see if we're being tailed. Order me a large black and get something for yourself that will tide you over until I can feed you."

The place was busy, filled to the brim with tourists getting their second wind and shoppers winding down. Nik stayed close while she inched her way along in the line toward the counter, but all the while, he kept his eyes on the door and on the passersby who were clearly visible through plate-glass windows on two sides of the coffee shop.

She'd just finished giving their order, when he muttered, "Shit."

"What?" J.C. started to turn toward him.

"No. Keep your eyes straight ahead." Then he turned and beamed a smile at the clerk behind the counter. "Cancel the drink order. We'll take two of the chocolate biscotti."

"For here or to go?" the clerk asked.

"To go." Nik handed her a twenty-dollar bill. "Keep the change."

The moment he had the biscotti in hand, he nudged J.C. toward the sizeable group of customers waiting for their specialty drinks. After weaving their way through the small crowd, he steered her down a short hall and through a doorway marked Employees Only. The brief glimpse of the room that she got on their dash toward the back door told her it was empty.

"You saw something," she said as Nik poked his head through the exit and scanned the alley.

"Call me paranoid, but a van just dropped off two men across the street, and they headed right for this place."

"Maybe they're addicted to the coffee."

"I hope you're right." Grabbing her hand, he pulled her into the alley and broke into a run. When they'd nearly reached the street, he stopped short. "Keep your back against the wall while I check it out."

After inching his way to the end of the alley, he peered carefully around the corner of the building, then swore under his breath again. "The van just turned the corner. Get behind the Dumpster."

An instant later, J.C. found herself pressed face-first against a metal Dumpster. The scent of garbage was ripe. Nik was at her back, so close that she felt it when he pulled out his gun.

Seconds ticked by. J.C. could feel the heat from Nik's body, but in spite of it, she shivered. "He's got an alibi. Why is he still after me?" she whispered.

"Shhhh." Nik squeezed her shoulder. "Don't fall apart on me now. We'll get through this. Could be the driver is just circling the block so that he can pick up the other two."

She heard the sudden rev of a motor as a vehicle turned slowly into the alley. So much for that idea. More seconds crawled by as the van drew closer, and J.C. prayed.

NIK COULD HEAR the crunching sounds of the tires moving over the debris on the floor of the alley. Then the van stopped—right in front of the Dumpster. His mind raced. Had one of those goons he'd spotted seen him going through the Employees Only door? If so, several scenarios ran through his mind. There were three of them, and it wouldn't be hard to block the exits to the alley. He and J.C. would be trapped and outnumbered.

A door opened. Was it the one that he and J.C. had used to leave the coffee shop?

The van moved forward a little and then stopped. If they started to search the alley, he'd have to create a disturbance so that J.C. could get away.

"Get ready," he whispered into her ear. "When I tell you to run, I want you to go as fast as you can to the end of the alley that the van just turned in from. Head back to the station and don't look back."

Another door opened. It sounded like the van. "You got them?" a gruff voice asked.

"No." The man replying had a high-pitched voice.

"You let them get away?"

"They must have spotted us and slipped out this way," the high-pitched voice replied. "Dickie had the front door covered."

"The boss is not going to be happy about this," the gruff voice said. "You're the shooting expert. You were supposed to take out the bodyguard and grab her as soon as they came out of the station."

"That damn reporter got in the way." The high-pitched voice grew whiny. "What were Dickie and I supposed to do? Get ourselves caught on film?"

"The boss doesn't like excuses. He wants her taken care of."

"They can't have gotten far. Maybe you're the one who let them get away."

"Get in the van," the gruff voice said. "We'll swing around and pick up Dickie. Then we'll find them and this time, you better not fail."

Listening to the van make its way toward the other end of the alley, Nik kept a tight rein on the emotions streaming through him. He was not going to think about what might have happened if he hadn't paid attention to his damn thumbs. If Carla Mitchell hadn't gotten in the way and the guy with the high-pitched voice had managed to shoot him, the three men would have J.C. right now. He could only imagine what she was feeling.

When the van finally moved out of the alley, he turned her around to face him.

"You were right," she said. "He's not going to stop. And that man would have killed you."

He tightened his grip on her. "We're going to stop them. You got that?"

He watched her gather herself in. "Yes. We're going to get them."

Nik grabbed her hand and together they ran for the other end of the alley. He scanned the street and spotted just what he was looking for. A package delivery truck from a company that promised on-time next-day delivery, and the driver was unloading.

Pointing to it, he said, "C'mon."

WITHIN MINUTES, J.C. found herself in the back of the truck wedged in between two columns of boxes. She was cold. In spite of the heat of the day, she'd begun to shiver, and there were goose bumps on her skin. But it was the icy ball of fear in her stomach that was numbing her.

In her mind she could still hear the words of the gruff voiced man in the alley. *You were supposed to take out the bodyguard.* It wasn't just the words, but the callous tone in which they were spoken that had her shivering again. He might have used the same tone to say, "You were supposed to bring the donuts." J.C. lifted her hands and saw that they were shaking. She'd nearly lost Nik.

And he was still standing in the street talking to the driver, his jacket pushed back so that his gun was visible, his thumbs tucked in the pockets of his jeans. He'd stood just that way in that little room in the church when he'd handcuffed her to the radiator. It was his intimidation pose.

And it was the wrong time to use it. He was still in plain sight if those goons in the van drove by.

"Slick," she called out. "You want to speed this up."

He sent a frown her way, then turned back to the driver. She watched as he pulled out his wallet, extracted several bills and passed them over to the man. The driver, pacified, gestured Nik inside, then began to transfer the boxes on his dolly to his truck. Nik, instead of climbing in the truck, pulled out his cell and continued to stand there like some sentinel on guard duty.

That was it. J.C. welcomed the anger because it melted the numbness. Scrambling to her feet, she moved to the back end of the truck. "Will you get in here? If those goons see you, you're going to get shot."

He leapt onto the truck, then turned, using his body to shield her from view, and continued to talk into his cell. She couldn't catch everything because of the traffic noises, but she heard him say "Cole." As soon as he pocketed his phone, he whirled, grabbed her by the arms and dragged her back into the little space she'd been crammed into before.

"I told you to stay put," he said. "Dammit, you were shaking like a leaf. You still are."

"I would have stayed put if you hadn't been standing out there in plain sight. Those men tried to shoot you. Because of me."

He gave her a shake. "And what do you think they had planned for you once they grabbed you."

"I nearly lost you." They spoke the words in unison. Then Nik pulled her close and covered her mouth with his. She tasted his fear as well as her own and she felt him tremble. Wrapping her arms around him, she drew him closer and poured everything she felt into the kiss.

WHEN NIK finally found the strength to draw back, they were on their knees facing each other in the cramped space. She wasn't shivering anymore, and neither was he.

With a sigh, J.C. snuggled her head against his shoulder. What had gone down in that alley had been a close call. And if Carla Mitchell hadn't been her usual dogged self, those men might have grabbed J.C. earlier.

No, if he allowed himself to dwell on that, he wouldn't be able to do his job. He heard the sounds of the doors at the back of the truck slamming shut. A moment later, he felt the driver climb in and the engine start. No, he wasn't going to dwell on what might have happened, and neither was J.C. He had a much better idea of how they might spend their time.

"Where are we going?" J.C. tightened her grip on him as the truck lurched into traffic.

"The St. Regis."

She drew back then to stare at him. "Why?"

"What if I said that I've asked Cole to get us a room so that we can make love all night long?"

He watched her eyes darken with desire just before they narrowed. "That's not the only reason, is it?"

Nik grinned at her as he ran his hands down her back to her hips, then drew her just a little closer. "No. I am going to make love to you. But I also have another agenda." He slipped his fingers beneath the waist of her jeans and felt the shiver move through her. "Just how good are you at multitasking?"

She lifted her chin. "Women are wired for multitasking. And caterers are pros at it."

"Too bad." He leaned forward and pressed his lips

to hers. "I was hoping we'd have to practice a bit." He pulled open the snap of her jeans.

"Nik?"

Her eyes had darkened to a deep emerald green. "I can't wait until we reach the hotel. I want you now." He gripped her hips to shift her so that her thighs straddled his. They were halfway back in the truck, completely surrounded by stacked boxes and cozy as sardines.

She pressed a hand against his chest. "You want to have sex in a delivery truck?"

"I do." He pulled her zipper down, and felt her skin tremble against the backs of his fingers. Then he slipped them deeper until he found her slick, wet heat. "I think you do, too. Don't you?"

J.C. FOUND SHE WANTED to more than anything. The icy cold that had gripped her moments ago was a dim memory, completely erased by the inferno of heat his touch was creating in her. "Do we have room?"

"Always questioning." He ran his mouth along the line of her jaw. "I love a challenge. Don't you?"

"Yes, I—" When he pushed two fingers into her, J.C. felt some of her brain cells begin to click off. "But…we were going to multitask."

"We are. But we should be able to go over my plan for the St. Regis while I'm inside of you." He nipped at the lobe of her ear and whispered, "You do want me inside of you, don't you?"

"Yes." She could feel herself already beginning to pulse around his fingers. Wrapping her arms around him, she dragged his mouth back to hers. "Time...do we have enough...?"

"We'll have to be fast." The urgency in his tone had all the other questions and objections slipping from her mind. Suddenly desperate, she pulled at the snap of his jeans.

"Not yet," he whispered against her lips. "First you have to turn around."

It took some doing, but she managed to squirm into a position so that she was kneeling in front of him and facing one of the boxes the driver had loaded to block them in. In the process, she'd managed to recall that they were supposed to be multitasking. "What's your plan once we get to the St. Regis?"

"Step one, we check in. Cole has a suite reserved for us." His hands gripped her jeans and dragged them down. Then his arms wrapped around her waist and she watched as he hooked his thumbs into the lacey elastic band of her briefs and lowered them to her knees. Just the sight of his hands moving on her skin had ripples of desire lashing through her. "And then?" she managed to ask.

The truck took a turn and he held her tight as they both shifted into the pile of boxes to their left.

"And then..." Once he'd steadied her again, his left hand moved slowly up the front of her thigh to the *V* between her legs. "I think I'll try this." She watched his middle finger slip into her fold and then press lightly against her clitoris. He wasn't rubbing it, just pressing much too gently. "Nik..."

"Do you want to know what we're going to do next at the St. Regis?"

"Yes." That was fast becoming a lie.

"Or do you want to know what I'm going to do to you next?"

"Yes." That was definitely a lie. She didn't want him to tell her. She just wanted him to do it.

For a moment, Nik didn't speak. Even the muted sounds of the traffic outside the truck seemed to fade. The only things she could hear were the snap of his jeans, the rasp of his zipper and the rustle of the denim against his skin. The noises were incredibly erotic. The sound of him tearing the foil from a condom nearly sent her over the edge.

When his finger traced her crack ever so lightly, the pulsing began deep inside of her, and she began to tremble.

"Do you have any idea what your response does to me?"

J.C. could only hope that it was half as devastating as what his touches and his words were doing to her. Gathering what brain cells she had left, she asked, "What's next?"

His arm tightened at her waist and he bent her over the box directly in front of her. "I think you know what I'm going to do to you next." He kissed the nape of her neck. "Why don't we just concentrate on that for a bit?"

"And…at the St. Regis?"

His laugh was a breath in her ear. "That's my girl," he murmured. "Focused to the last. We're going to ask to see the ballroom. Any other questions?"

Before she could answer, the truck lurched again, flattening them both against the top of the box he'd bent her over. Reaching behind, she gripped his buttock with her hand. "I want you inside of me now."

"That's one order I don't mind following." He entered her, filling her, stretching her. She cried out at the huge wave of pleasure.

The truck lurched again, and he thrust even deeper.

"Sorry," he murmured in her ear as he withdrew and thrust in again. "I intended to take you slowly. But my plans have changed. Hold on."

She did hold on—one hand gripping the edge of the box, the other holding fast to his buttock. "Fast would be...good."

Nik increased the pace. At the same time, he began to rub his finger against her clitoris. When he bit her shoulder, she felt her climax rip through her.

"Last step," Nik whispered hoarsely as he thrust one final time.

15

As Nik drew her into the lobby of the St. Regis, J.C. was immediately aware that she was underdressed. The marble columns and floor didn't go with her jeans and T-shirt. Neither did the crystal chandelier nor the huge vase of real flowers that graced the carved oak table in the center of the room.

"I need some clothes." Her gaze lingered on the displays in one of the exclusive shops that lined the lobby.

"We'll get to it," Nik assured her. "First we're going to check in. I had Cole make the reservations." He paused right by the carved oak table and in plain sight of everyone, he kissed her hand and smiled at her. "Before we get on with this, tell me how you are."

"Fine," she said.

He lowered his voice. "Any bruises? That was a pretty rough ride."

She felt the heat stain her cheeks. "Any bruises would be worth it."

He grinned at her. "Yes, they would." He tucked a strand of hair behind her ear. "That was fun. We'll have to try it again someday."

Much to her surprise, she found herself agreeing. In addition to being one of the most erotic experiences she'd ever had, making love with Nik in the back of a delivery truck *had* been fun. She narrowed her eyes.

"What?" he asked.

"You're not what I first thought you'd be."

"I'm not?"

J.C. shook her head as she recalled the first time she'd seen him, totally focused, totally serious and very dangerous-looking as he'd stood over the body in the sacristy. "I can't quite reconcile the man I first saw with the man I just had…"

He leaned down and whispered in her ear. "Down-and-dirty sex with in the back of a delivery truck?"

"Yes."

"What if I told you that I'm having a little trouble adjusting to him, too?"

"Really?"

He raised her hand to his lips again. "Jude Catherine, that was a first for me."

You're a first for me. Nik wasn't quite comfortable with the thought as he drew her toward the registration desk, but for now he pushed the discomfort aside. They'd come here for information. "When we register, just play along with me."

"What exactly are we doing? You only gave me the vaguest outline of what your plan is."

"I want to see that ballroom where the charity ball took place. Perhaps it will give us an idea of how our Frankie boy managed to be in two places at once." That was part one of his plan. For the other part—well they both needed a break. And he intended to give her what he hadn't given her in the van.

He squeezed her hand. "Just follow my lead. We're about to have some more fun."

"Ah." She grinned at him. "More multitasking?"

"May I help you?" The woman whose name tag read Lara beamed a smile at them.

"Arthur Varden," Nik said.

Lara tapped some keys, then her smile brightened. "Ah, yes, my manager said that you're interested in planning a destination wedding." She punched a number into a phone and said, "Mr. Varden is here," then turned back to Nick. "The ballroom manager asked to be notified as soon as you arrived, Mr. Varden." She tapped a few more keys. "Your personal assistant phoned just a short while ago. Your suite should be ready shortly. If you'd like, you could check your luggage with the bellman."

"We don't have any," Nik was surprised to hear J.C. say. "We made the plane in Philly. Our luggage didn't. The airline has promised to deliver it tonight. But…" She spread her hands.

Lara's smile turned sympathetic. "I'm sure you can find whatever you need for this evening in one of our gift shops. We even have a personal shopper if you'd like to make out a list." She passed a pen and a notepad to J.C. and another to Nik.

"Excuse me." Lara moved to speak to the man who'd appeared in the doorway behind her.

"A personal shopper?" she hissed. "What do we do?"

"Go ahead and fill it out," Nik suggested. "We're staying the night."

At her raised eyebrows, he said, "I can't risk taking you back to Aunt Cass's place. Cole Buchanan is the only one who knows we're here. And it's the last place anyone would think to look for us."

"Right." J.C. turned her attention to the list. "So for tonight we're Arthur Varden and…? What's my name, by the way? And how rich are we? I need to know what we can afford. And if we're planning a wedding, we must be engaged." She raised a hand and wiggled her bare fingers at him. "I think I need a diamond."

Nik shook his head. "I'm beginning to think I've created a monster. And you can pick your own name. Cole picked out Arthur Varden for me."

"Hmmm." She tapped her pen against her bottom lip. "I think I'll be…Carrie."

"Carrie?"

"She was my favorite on *Sex and the City.*" She began to scribble away on the list.

Nik simply stared at her. "You're really getting into this, aren't you?"

"Mmmm," she murmured as she continued to write.

Admiration filled him. She had to be the most re-silient woman he'd ever met. Less than an hour ago, she'd been with him behind that Dumpster, listening to two thugs discuss why one of them had failed to shoot him and grab her. Then when he'd wanted her in that truck, when he'd needed her, she'd given herself so generously to him. He didn't know anyone braver. And now, here she was throwing herself fully into the little charade that he'd set up. He'd never met anyone like her.

And he was falling in love with her. The realization hit him like a blow to his solar plexus. For a moment all he knew was that he was numb, and he couldn't latch on to one coherent thought because his head was spinning. It was still revolving when a man's voice said his name. "Mr. Varden?"

"Hmmm?" It took him a second to realize that the short, balding man to his right was talking to him.

"Welcome to the St. Regis."

Gathering his thoughts, Nik shook the man's hand.

"I'm Howard Melnitz, the banquet manager. Your personal assistant, Mr. Buchanan, told me you'd be arriving and that you're thinking of having the St. Regis help you plan your destination wedding. How can I be of service?"

There was a short beat of silence while Nik still tried to get it together.

J.C. shot him a look, then smiled at Howard Melnitz. "I'm Carrie Manning, Artie's fiancée. If you wouldn't mind, we'd like to see your grand ballroom. I've heard such raves about it."

"Are you sure you wouldn't like to settle in your room first?"

She smiled at him. "Heavens, no. When we get into our room, you won't be able to get us out. I always like to take care of business before pleasure, if you get my drift, Mr. Melnitz?"

"Why, yes, I think I do, Ms. Manning."

Nik could have sworn that Howard Melnitz was blushing.

J.C. turned to Lara. "I've jotted down a few things, just some essentials to tide us over until our luggage arrives. Perhaps your personal shopper could gather them together and send them up to our room?"

"Happy to," Lara said.

J.C. beamed a smile at Melnitz as she slipped her arm through his. "Shall we go?"

"IT'S LOVELY," J.C. said as she took in the elegant room.

"The St. Regis is one of the oldest and most exclusive hotels in San Francisco. The ballroom itself has been featured in *Architectural Digest*." He moved away to one of the walls. "These sconces were made in Europe and sent here by boat. As you can tell from the slight variations in the carving on the finials along the balcony, the whole railing is hand-carved. You can't find that kind of work in the newer hotels."

"No. How many can you seat in the ballroom?"

"Four hundred. Five hundred if we use the mezzanine."

J.C. glanced up at the railing that formed a balcony on three sides of the room. Her stomach plummeted as she realized that anyone seated at them could indeed be seen from any place in the lower ballroom.

As Melnitz led the way down the room, she lowered her voice and spoke to Nik. "Notice the way the tables are arranged on the mezzanine?"

"Yeah." They were deep and angled so that two of the people seated at them could be seen from below only in profile. "Frankie would have been in plain view."

"Yeah. But only from a distance."

"Ms. Manning?"

"Yes, Mr. Melnitz?"

"I can offer you a dance floor in two sizes—medium or large, depending on how much dancing you plan on providing."

"Oh, I'll need the large dance floor. My Artie here is half-Greek. We'll be cutting up a rug, as they say."

"Very good, Ms. Manning. Is there anything else you want to know about the ballroom?"

She glanced up at the mezzanine. "I believe there is. Artie, can you do me a favor?"

"Anything, darling."

"Would you go up to the balcony and sit at one of the tables with Mr. Melnitz? I'd like to get a sense of whether or not the guests on the mezzanine feel like they're part of the whole celebration or if they'll feel left out. Would that be all right, Mr. Melnitz?"

"Of course, but we've never had a complaint about any guests feeling left out. Why we had a charity ball just last night and everyone felt included. In fact, one of the cochairs sat up here with her husband and a few friends."

"We'll just humor the little lady, Mr. Melnitz," Nik said. "How do we get up there?"

"Right this way."

A few moments later, Nik and Melnitz appeared on the mezzanine. Nik sat at one of the tables and called down to her. "What do you think, darling?"

"I think it's going to be just fine," J.C. said. She could hardly wait until they rejoined her on the main floor. Slipping her arm through Nik's, she turned to the banquet manager. "Thank you so much, Mr. Melnitz. You've given us a lot to consider. Artie and I want to be married in a place where we can share our joy with our friends, and so far I'm impressed. We'll want to discuss it and sleep on it, of course. Will you be around in the morning?"

"Of course, Ms. Manning. Is there anything else I

can show you—the hotel dining rooms, the fitness room, other guest rooms?"

"No, I'm sure we're going to get a sense of the St. Regis during our stay."

Melnitz nodded. "The Sheridan Suite is one of our finest. Mr. Varden's personal assistant insisted."

"I can't wait...unless...Artie, do you want to see anything else?"

Nik shook his head. "I'm fine if you are, darling."

"Good," J.C. said, drawing him toward the door.

The moment they were alone in the elevator, she said, "I know how Frankie could have done it. He used a doppelganger."

"A doppelganger?"

"A look-alike. I'm betting he hired someone who looked like him to attend the charity ball with Gina while he took care of his business at St. Peter's Church."

Nik thought for a minute. "That would certainly explain how he could be in two places at once. But it sure as hell would be risky. What if someone who knew him figured out the hoax?"

"Gina Carlucci was one of the cochairs. I've learned enough from watching my stepmother do this kind of stuff to know that the men are just the window dressing. They provide the escort on the night of the event. That's all. As a cochair, Gina could have made sure that their table was up on that balcony in plain sight, but far enough away that no one could see Frankie up close. I'll bet if you ask Captain Parker, the only place he saw Frankie last night was at that table on the mezzanine."

"And people see what they expect to see," Nik mused softly.

"Exactly. The others at their table could have been in on it or they could have been strangers who wouldn't have known that they were eating and talking with a stand-in. What do you think?"

He took her hands then, very reluctant to wipe the look of excitement off of her face. "I think that I really like the way your mind works. But it's only a theory. We don't have any proof."

"I know. But we can ask my parents tomorrow at the garden party just when and under what circumstances they actually saw Frankie at that charity ball. I know that's how he did it."

"Me, too." He smiled at her then. "My thumbs have been prickling ever since you said the word *doppelganger*."

The elevator door opened and he drew her toward the double set of doors at the end of a short hallway. "But right now, why don't we agree to leave Nik Angelis, Jude Catherine Riley and all our troubles and worries behind?" He stuck the magnetic card into the slot, then opened the door. "For one night we're going to be Arthur Varden and his fiancée, Carrie Manning. And we're going to enjoy all the amenities that the St. Regis has to offer."

Scooping her up in his arms, he carried her over the threshold and into the Sheridan Suite.

A HALF HOUR LATER, Nik glanced around the main room of the suite. He'd never consciously tried to give a woman romance before. A good time, yes. But romance had always been Theo's or Kit's gig. And truth be told, as he glanced at the tapered candles burning on the grand piano and on nearly every table in the room, he felt a bit uncomfortable with the "ambience."

The hotel staff had been very helpful. Room service had suggested a menu, and the waiter had provided the candles, along with the flowers and the chilled champagne. The waiter had even turned the radio to a classics station, and Debussy now spilled softly into the room. Nik hoped that J.C. would like it.

He'd showered quickly and was grateful to find that the hotel's personal shopper had sent up a fresh change of underwear along with the toiletries that J.C. had jotted down on the list. And though he felt a bit foolish in it, he'd slipped into one of the robes that had been hanging in the closet.

He was pretty sure that Artie would have worn the robe. Running a hand through his hair, he began to pace. Where in the hell had Cole gotten that ridiculous name anyway? But if it would take J.C.'s mind off the fact that a crazy man was out to kill her, he'd be anyone for one night. Try as he might, he couldn't forget the way her eyes had looked when he'd first turned her around to face him in that alley. He'd seen fear and a vulnerability that she did her best to hide.

Tonight, he wasn't going to let her think about any of that. As for tomorrow? He was going to make damn sure that Frankie boy didn't even think of making a move on J.C. at that garden party. If he did, it might very well be his last move.

Glancing at his watch, Nik frowned. She'd been in that bathroom for a long time. Maybe he should go in....

No. He'd seen the huge sunken tub in the bathroom

and he imagined that she'd opted to indulge in that amenity rather than a quick shower. He might even have joined her, but he'd wanted to get in a quick call to Cole Buchanan. It was a long shot, but Cole was going to check with some casting agencies on the off chance that Frankie Carlucci had hired an actor for his little charade.

Cole was making progress on the financials, too. Frankie boy had run up some gambling debts, and he owed some very bad people in Vegas. It wasn't proof. But in detective work, you had to content yourself with gathering nails, one by one, until you had enough to pound the lid on the coffin.

Turning toward the door to the suite's other bedroom, Nik once more debated going in there. What in the world was she doing?

J.C. TOOK A LONG LOOK in the mirror. It wasn't that the hotel's personal shopper hadn't gotten her what she'd ordered. It was the fact that she was short. The lace teddy was okay, but the robe that went with it dragged on the floor.

She let the robe drop to the floor. Better. Her hair, she couldn't do much about. The steam from the bath she'd taken had activated the curls. She'd piled it on top of her head and tried to get a few of them to "artfully" escape. The end result was that her head looked like a mop. Pulling out the ribbon, she let her hair fall to her shoulders, and studied the image in the mirror.

The nerves in her stomach knotted even tighter. This was the best she was going to do. She might pretend that she was Carrie Manning for a night, but underneath, she was J.C. Riley, and she'd never set out to intentionally seduce a man before. At least not the way she wanted to seduce Nik tonight.

Pressing a hand against her stomach, she drew in a breath and let it out. Tonight she didn't want to be Nik Angelis's sex buddy. She wanted to be his lover.

So. She looked herself straight in the eye. "You can do this. You got through culinary school. You got away from three killers today. Pretend you're Carrie Manning if you have to. But you're going to do this."

Turning, she walked to the door, opened it and then stopped short on the threshold. She was aware of the flicker of candlelight, the gleam of silver on a table set for two and the music. But her eyes never left Nik. His eyes were darker than she'd ever seen them. He'd set this stage for her. The sweetness of the gesture had her heart taking a long, slow tumble.

She loved him. What she hadn't been able to admit in the back of that truck, she had no choice but to admit now. The scariness of the realization, and the joy of it, sang through her more potently than wine. And suddenly, she knew that she could seduce him. She didn't have to pretend to be anyone but herself.

NIK COULDN'T MOVE. The moment J.C. appeared in the doorway, all he could do was look at her and absorb. A cream-colored bit of lace and silk skimmed her breasts and fell to her thighs. And her hair was down. In the candlelight, the tumble of curls glinted with hints of fire. And her eyes. He'd never seen them that dark before. Was it his imagination or could he see a reflection of his own emotions in them?

She smiled and walked toward him then. He thanked the Fates for that because he still couldn't move. As she drew closer, all he was aware of was her. She filled him, pushing everything else out.

When she placed a hand on his chest right where the robe formed a *V,* he felt his heartbeat quicken.

"I'm going to seduce you."

Didn't she know that she already had? Couldn't she tell? He felt the tug at his waist as she pulled his belt loose, the brush of the robe as it slid off his shoulders and fell to the floor. And still he couldn't find the strength to move.

She was beautiful. He'd thought her cute and even pretty at times. Why hadn't he seen that she was beautiful? There was a pressure tightening around his heart.

"You're beautiful," she said.

"No, that's you," he answered. His voice sounded breathless.

"Yeah, right." She ran her hands over his shoulders and down his arms. "The first time I saw you, I thought of Adonis, a man beautiful enough to have two goddesses vying for his favors. I'd never really understood that myth until you first made love to me. You're a man women would fight over. You're a man I'd fight for."

Her fingers left a trail of fire and ice as they danced down his chest. He sucked in his breath sharply when they reached his waist and toyed with the band of elastic there.

J.C. glanced up at him and smiled. "The hotel's personal shopper has good taste. Too bad you won't be wearing them for long." She knelt down then and drew him with her to the floor. Then framing his face with her hands, she brought his mouth to hers.

Any minute now, he would regain control, Nik thought as her lips whispered over his. But the pleasure she gave him was so sweet, so drugging, that he didn't want to end it. Not yet. Not ever. Each nip of her teeth, each brush of her tongue, made his blood thicken and move more slowly. It was agonizing. Magnificent. His skin grew damp, hot. His breath backed up in his lungs and burned.

He wasn't even aware of the moment when she pushed him to the floor and straddled his waist. Her mouth still moved over him, and the lace, the silk, the flesh that was her rubbed against his skin until desire flared hot and deep in his center.

Still, he couldn't move. He was helpless, trapped in the sensations that only she could bring him.

IT WAS SO EASY, J.C. thought. Why had she worried that she wouldn't be able to do this? Was it knowing that she loved him that made the difference?

She'd felt that softening, that instant of complete surrender as she'd pushed him onto his back and straddled him. And it had empowered her as well as aroused her. When his hands moved to her waist, she pushed them away. She wasn't done with him, not yet. She continued to move her hands and mouth over him, determined to know more. To have more.

She pressed her lips against the pulse thudding in the hollow of his throat. That made his breath catch. She moved her tongue over his nipple. That made him sigh. She lifted one of his hands, nibbled on his fingers and wrenched a moan out of him when she nipped his thumb.

Moving lower, she slipped her fingers beneath the elastic of his briefs, then lowered them slowly, following the path with her teeth and tongue until…

When her mouth closed over him, Nik felt the strength finally return to his limbs. Arching up, he took her face gently in his hands and eased her away. Now that he could move again, he had to firmly strap down his control. He found the robe and drew out the condom. When she took it from him and sheathed him with it herself, he very nearly lost it.

Teetering on the edge of orgasm, he hooked an arm around her waist and dragged her beneath him. Arms trembling as he braced himself above her, he stared down. Her chin was lifted, but what he saw in her eyes was such a perfect match to what he was feeling that he was able to gather his control once more and slip into her slowly. Eyes locked, hands linked, they began to move together. There was only her face in the candlelight, only her hair burning bright on the rug, only her body moving faster and faster in perfect rhythm with his.

Only J.C., he thought as desire turned white-hot and the flash fire took them both.

16

"IF I NEVER GO TO another garden party, it will be too soon," Nik said as Theo and Sam Schaeffer joined him at one of the bars that had been set up at intervals along the lawn.

Theo laughed, a rich sound that merged into the chatter of guests and the soft melodies of a string quartet playing at the far end of the pool. Nik's remark even drew a smile from the usually sober Sam Schaeffer.

The two had arrived thirty minutes earlier and had very skillfully made the rounds. It never ceased to impress Nik that his brother could fit in so easily in these kinds of sophisticated surroundings. Of course, Theo had much more experience at these kind of functions. During the three years his brother spent in the D.A.'s office before he'd left to open his practice as a defense attorney, he'd had to accompany his boss to a lot of political functions. But from the looks of it, Theo had taken to the social stuff like a fish to water. He must have spent ten minutes talking to J.C.'s older brothers. Nik had found them a bit stuffy, but Theo had looked perfectly at ease with them. In fact, it looked to him as though his brother was actually enjoying himself.

Mentally, he shook his head. "There isn't even any decent food." Nik returned his gaze to J.C., who stood about ten feet away shaking hands with the latest young man her stepmother had introduced her to. Cole Buchanan and Pepper Rossi were selecting food from a table nearby, and Pepper's brothers, Matt and Luke, were just a little farther away near the pool.

Handling security at an outdoor party was not a piece of cake by any means, and Nik wanted it over. He wanted to take J.C. away right now and feed her. She hadn't had a bite to eat since they'd arrived, and she'd only picked at her breakfast at the hotel. Neither of them had brought up what had happened between them during the night.

There was so much he wanted to say, needed to say. So much he wasn't sure he would ever find the right words. He was in love with her, and there were moments during the night that he was sure that he'd seen the same feelings in her eyes. But he wanted words. And it had been the wrong time to press for them. He'd wanted her safe first.

Not that he was sure that she was safe here. He scanned the grounds again. The lawns were spacious, the pool area carefully landscaped, as were the tennis courts beyond.

He'd had a bad feeling ever since they'd arrived, and in spite of the fact that he knew that J.C. was being guarded by the best, his thumbs hadn't given him a break. He'd wanted the damn party over from the moment Alicia Hensen Riley had eased J.C. away from him for a private talk.

He'd used the opportunity to quiz the mayor about

whether or not he'd had any personal time with Frankie Carlucci at the charity ball. J.C. had been right. The only time her father had seen Frankie was at the table on that balcony.

Nik had managed to rejoin J.C. several times since then only to have her stepmother step in and draw her away on some pretext or other. J.C. had warned him that her duties at the party would include meeting and greeting a series of eligible bachelors that her parents would lob at her like so many tennis balls. By Nik's count the blond, preppy one she was currently smiling at was bachelor number four. Under other circumstances he might have been jealous, but he was too damn worried for that.

Theo nudged him in the side. "Check out a new arrival at nine o'clock."

Nik shifted his gaze to the side of the house and saw Michael Dano shaking hands with the mayor. At his side were Mario's wife, Deanna, and her son, Eddie. Like Theo, Michael Dano seemed to fit right in at the party. Nik was willing to bet that the man would be Alicia Hensen Riley's choice for bachelor number five. "What are they doing here?"

"I imagine they're representing the Oliver family. The Olivers have always been loyal supporters of Mayor Riley," Theo replied. "Roman can't be here, Mario won't leave the hospital, and Sadie and Juliana are missing. It looks as though Michael, Mrs. Oliver and her son are stepping in to fill the gap."

Nik's eyes never left Michael. "Dano's been with them how long?"

"Three years," Theo said.

"What do you know about him?"

"I met him for the first time when Sam and I were at the hospital this morning."

He turned to Theo. "Were you able to talk to Roman?"

"No. I'll be going back this afternoon. But the surgery was successful. The doctors are optimistic that he'll make a complete recovery."

"Good news." Nik allowed himself to savor it for a moment. "And the bad news is he'll be charged today, won't he?"

Theo said nothing. There wasn't anything to say. He and Kit needed to come up with some clue that might point the investigation in a different direction. So far Cole and the Rossis hadn't uncovered anything useful in the financials of the two families. It didn't help that they'd had to interrupt their work to come to a garden party to provide security for J.C.

The mayor and his wife were now greeting Captain Parker and Commissioner Galvin. When a waiter paused and offered a selection of fancy finger foods, Nik shook his head, and Theo selected a toast point with—Nik suppressed a shudder—caviar. "I bet if they'd let J.C. cater it, she'd have drummed up something more substantial than finger sandwiches and fish eggs on toast." At Mayor Riley's insistence, he'd tried the caviar earlier, and not even the crisp and fruity chardonnay the bartender had recommended had been up to the task of washing the flavor away.

"Actually, the caviar is quite good," Theo remarked. "So is the wine."

Nik met Sam Schaeffer's eyes and awarded Sam points when the young man rolled his. At least there was someone at this shindig who agreed with him. Though why Theo had brought his intern to a social event was something that Nik wanted to ask him.

"Sam here prefers the food that Dad serves at The Poseidon."

So Theo had taken his intern to The Poseidon, too. Mentally, Nik raised his eyebrows, more curious than ever about Theo's intern. They seemed to be joined at the hip.

"Actually, people never come to these things for the food," Sam said. "They come either to be seen or to watch."

Nik studied Sam. It was the most the young man had said since Theo had introduced him in Parker's office. There was something vaguely familiar about him. Now that he thought about it, Nik was almost sure that he'd seen those intelligent brown eyes before, and there was something in the cadence of the way he spoke…but he couldn't jar the memory loose. "You've been to a few of these, I gather."

Sam wrinkled his nose. "More than a few. I try to survive by people watching. J.C. is talking right now to Hale Dashwood."

"Uh-huh." Nik flicked a look in J.C.'s direction. "And he would be?"

"A soap-opera star who's just made the transition to big-screen stardom. He played the second lead in Bruce Willis's last film, and he's here in San Francisco filming a romantic comedy with Jennifer Lopez. So he's on the A-list when it comes to parties. It's a real coup that the Rileys got him to come."

Though Theo was discreet, Nik didn't miss it when

his brother laid a hand on Sam's arm and the young man shut up. Nik might have pushed the conversation further just to see what would happen if he hadn't been interrupted by his aunt Cass's arrival.

"I'm late," she said in a breathless voice, adjusting the straw hat that was threatening to slip off of her head. "Fashionably so, I hope."

Because he was closer, Theo hugged his aunt first. "What a lovely surprise. I didn't expect to see you here, Aunt Cass."

Nik was surprised, too. As far as he knew the only person in their family who was on the "A-list" was Theo.

Cass pressed a hand against her chest and drew in a breath. "Alicia Hensen Riley is a new client, and she invited me to come just this morning. I had to rush to get myself together, and then I had to help Helena pack."

"Helena pack?" Nik and Theo spoke in unison.

Nik could have sworn that Cass blushed.

"Oh, my. I wasn't supposed to say anything. I promised."

"She's decided to go back to Greece?" Theo asked.

"I thought she and Dad had sorted things out," Nik said. "They looked happy enough when they ran out of the restaurant in the middle of the lunch hour rush."

"They were back dancing up a storm last night," Sam added.

"She's not going back to Greece," Cass said. "I can tell you that much. At least not anytime soon."

Nik watched his aunt's eyes darken. "Maybe for their…" She cut herself off by placing the palm of her hand over her mouth. Then dropping her hand, she glanced around the lawn. "I have to find Mrs. Riley. I think she's worried about J.C." Cass placed her free hand on Nik's arm. "But I think everything will be just fine."

Nik frowned as he glanced around the party, too, but there was nothing untoward happening, nothing that indicated anything was going on other than a boring social function that people attended to either see or be seen. However, *think* wasn't the word he wanted to hear from his aunt. He wanted her to say she *knew* that everything would be fine.

His damn thumbs were burning now, and he was pretty sure that something bad was about to go down.

It was then that he spotted the mayor and his wife, hurrying forward, hands extended to a couple who had just stepped around the corner of the house.

Frankie and Gina Carlucci had arrived.

"Shit." He'd taken one step forward when Commissioner Galvin and D.C. Parker stepped directly into his path.

J.C. BARELY SUPPRESSED a yawn as she continued to smile at bachelor number four, Hale Dashwood. That couldn't be his real name. It occurred to her that "Arthur Varden" would suit him to a *T,* and she barely kept herself from laughing. She could feel Nik's eyes on her, and while she knew that Cole Buchanan and Pepper Rossi were standing only a few feet away, it was the fact that Nik was watching her that made her feel secure.

She'd really hated leaving the hotel this morning. There was so much that she needed to say to him, so much she needed to hear him say.

But for the moment, she didn't dare take her focus from Hale. Instinct, honed by years of experience with the type of man Alicia always sent her way, told her that Hale liked to be the center of attention.

"Your parents throw a lovely party."

"Yes, they do."

"I'm new at this game, myself. But once I got the film with Bruce Willis, the invites just kept rolling in. The problem is I never know quite what to talk about. My publicist says I need to brush up on my small-talk skills."

J.C. tuned Hale Dashwood out. She couldn't help but wonder if he'd chosen acting as a career so that he could escape from himself by pretending to be other, much more interesting, characters. Of course, it would help if she could drink the wine that she was holding in her hand, but she didn't dare. Not on an empty stomach.

When was the party going to be over?

"…had to hire three different stunt doubles when I took that fall out of the helicopter with Bruce."

"What?" J.C. asked, suddenly tuning back in.

"I couldn't do the stunt because I have this thing with heights. I've been in therapy but—"

J.C. grabbed his arm. She barely kept herself from shaking him. "I want to know about the stunt-double part. Who hired them? Where did they hire them?"

Hale beamed a smile at her. "Funny you should ask. Last party I went to someone wanted to know about stunt doubles, too. I guess you never know just what will make a conversational hit at one of these affairs."

"No scenes," D.C. Parker muttered under his breath to Nik. "The Carluccis are here as guests of the mayor."

"You knew they were coming?" Nik asked.

"No, I didn't," Parker said. "But I'm not surprised."

Nik glanced over to where J.C. was still talking to the A-list movie star, Hal Something-or-other, and satisfied himself that Cole Buchanan was close by. The Carluccis were still chatting with their hosts.

"I'm going to the hospital right after we take our leave of the mayor," Parker said to Theo. "I've held off longer than I should have."

Shit, Nik thought as he swung his gaze to his brother. To his surprise, he saw that Theo once more had placed a hand on Sam Schaeffer's arm. The young man looked very pale. Why?

Something was flickering at the edge of his mind when his aunt's laugh distracted him. He glanced over to see that she and Commissioner Galvin were holding hands. His aunt Cass was blushing again, and she looked somehow younger.

First his father and Helena, and now his aunt and the commissioner? What in hell was going on with his family?

J.C. FELT THE little spurt of adrenaline and she tightened her grip on Hale's hand. "Do you remember who asked you about stunt doubles?"

Hale's smile faded a bit. "Not really. These parties are such a crush. And I'm not good with names."

It's probably hard to remember other people's names when you're so focused on yourself, she thought. "Was it a man or a woman?"

"A man."

"Can you describe him?"

Hale's smile brightened again. "Sure. Character study is my strong suit. He walked with sort of a swagger, and he had longish hair. A lot like the way I wore mine in my soap days, but I thought he was a bit old for the style."

"How old?"

"Oh, late thirties, early forties. The wife was younger. I'd say in her early twenties. Very attractive if you like the blond-bimbo type. A lot of men do. Now my type is more—"

J.C. tightened her grip on his hand. "What else do you remember about the man who asked you about stunt doubles?"

Hale frowned in concentration. "Well-dressed. I asked him for the name of his tailor. The jacket was real snakeskin, I think, and he had a nice diamond on his pinky. Not my style, but I complimented him on it, and that's when he asked about hiring stunt doubles."

J.C. wondered if Nik's thumbs were pricking. "Did you tell him where he could hire one?"

"Yeah. Why not. Might as well spread the wealth. My publicist says—"

Once again, J.C. stifled the urge she had to shake him. "Who did you send him to?"

"I gave him the name of the best casting outfit in L.A. You should see the double they hired for me. Almost identical."

J.C. couldn't help but think of fate. What were the chances that she would run into Hale Dashwood and he would hand her the key to putting Frankie Carlucci behind bars?

"WELL, IT'S SUCH a lovely surprise to have run into you, Chad," Cass said.

Chad, Nik thought with a frown. His aunt and Galvin had only met three minutes ago and they were already on a first-name basis. And Commissioner Galvin still hadn't released Cass's hand.

He liked that about as much as he liked the fact that J.C. was now holding the A-list movie star's hand. Out of the corner of his eye he saw Alicia Hensen Riley approaching J.C. Good, he thought. It must be time for bachelor number five. Just as he'd thought, she had Michael Dano in tow.

"I really must speak to my hostess," Cass continued, "and let her know that I've finally arrived. I'm so late."

Nik glanced over to the spot where he'd last seen the mayor talking to the Carluccis. He stiffened and scanned the lawn when he saw Mayor Riley and Frankie still talking, but there was no sign of Gina.

"Nonsense," Galvin was saying. "The garden party lasts for another hour. We've arrived in prime time, so to speak. C'mon, I have to speak to my hostess, also."

Hand in hand, Cass and Galvin walked toward J.C., Mrs. Riley, the movie star and Dano.

"Your commissioner moves fast," Theo murmured.

He sure as hell does, Nik thought.

"It reminded me a bit of that scene in *Romeo and Juliet* when the two kids first meet at the Capulets' party," Sam said.

D.C. Parker chuckled. "I can vouch for Galvin's character, guys." Then he spoke in a lower voice to Nik. "Be nice now. The mayor and Frankie are headed our way."

"I want to get J.C. out of here," Nik replied.

"Even if you're right about him," Parker said in the same low tone that only Nik could hear, "Frankie won't try anything here. Too many people would see it."

Nik recalled the mezzanine at the St. Regis's grand ballroom. This is exactly when Frankie would make his move, he thought. Right now when he had the perfect alibi.

"CASSANDRA ANGELIS, you already know Alicia," Commissioner Galvin said, "but I'd like to introduce my niece and godchild, Jude Catherine Riley."

J.C. stifled her impatience as she held out her hands to Nik's aunt. She had to get to Nik and tell him what she knew. But he was talking with Frankie and her dad, and she couldn't very well tell Nik with Frankie standing right there. They'd need to contact the casting company in L.A. and get the proof first.

"It's such a pleasure to finally meet you," Cass Angelis said.

Once the older woman's hands closed over hers, J.C. felt her nerves begin to settle. For the first time since she'd left the hotel with Nik that morning, the ball of fear in her stomach eased, and she had the sudden impression that she and Cass were alone in the garden.

"Nik is a good man," Cass said.

"Yes." J.C. nodded.

"He doesn't have the spit and polish of Theo or the sweetness of Kit." Cass squeezed J.C.'s hands. "But he takes care of his own. You can trust him."

She could, J.C. realized. And she did. Nik had told her that his aunt Cass had special powers. It wasn't that she hadn't believed him, but she hadn't realized what that could mean until now.

The moment that Cass released her hands, J.C. was once more aware of the string music and the chatter of voices. She returned her uncle Chad's hug, then turned to find Cass holding her mother's hands. J.C. had the impression that her mother was experiencing that sense of stillness that she'd just experienced.

"She's quite amazing," Uncle Chad said. "When she took my hands a few minutes ago, it was as if certain things that I'd been thinking about and putting off just fell into place."

Was that what had happened to her, J.C. wondered.

"It will be fine," Cass said as she released Alicia's hands.

J.C. noted that her stepmother didn't seem quite that convinced.

"We need to talk some more," Alicia said in a brisk voice. Then she turned to J.C. "Jude Catherine, could you go up to the kitchen and ask the caterer to bring out more food? The tables need to be replenished, and I really need to talk to Cass for a moment longer."

"Sure." J.C. glanced over, intending to signal Nik to join her, but Frankie Carlucci and her father blocked her view of him for the moment. Her news would certainly keep, she thought as she hurried toward the porch steps. She was halfway up when one of the waitstaff pushed through the back door.

"Excuse me, miss."

J.C. stepped back to let him pass her with a loaded tray. It would seem that the caterer was already on top of things, and for a moment, she debated even completing her errand. A glance over her shoulder told her Cole and Pepper hadn't followed her. They'd moved to a line of trees at the edge of the lawn and they seemed to be deep in conversation with the two men Cole Buchanan had introduced earlier as Luke and Matt Rossi. She knew that the two Rossi brothers had been assigned to mingle with the guests and keep an eye out for anyone who looked suspicious, as well as for possible snipers. They were probably reporting in.

Well, she'd deliver Alicia's message quickly. Surely, she'd be safe in her own home. Especially, since Frankie boy was otherwise occupied for the moment. As the porch door swung shut behind her, J.C. took a moment to let her eyes adjust. After the bright sunshine in the garden, the back hallway was dark. Through an archway straight ahead, she could see two of the wait-staff loading trays and wondered again at the errand that Alicia had sent her on. The caterer seemed to have everything under control.

She was turning to go back outside when Gina Carlucci stepped out of the shadows and pressed a gun into her side.

17

"WE'RE GOING TO WALK through the kitchen and go out the front door," Gina said in her breathy Marilyn Monroe voice. "And don't even think of screaming or I'll shoot one of the waiters. You wouldn't want me to do that, would you?"

J.C. felt fear settle into a ball in her stomach. Gina was standing close enough that she could read the truth of what she'd just said in her eyes. "You're not going to get away with this."

From the garden, she heard a scream, followed by shouts.

"Move," Gina whispered softly. "Your bodyguards are going to be busy for the next few minutes. A little girl just fell into the pool. Those big brave men won't want her to drown."

Gina was right. Nik, Cole and the rest of the Rossis would be heading right for the pool. J.C.'s mind was racing as they moved through the kitchen. Gina stuck close, concealing the gun with a sweater she'd thrown over her arm. No one paid them any heed. J.C. couldn't even catch anyone's eye. Nik, she thought, I hope your thumbs are falling off.

They made it out of the house and halfway across

the lawn faster than J.C. would have liked, so she stumbled and fell to one knee.

"Uh, uh, uh," Gina breathed. "No tricks. Get up and keep moving unless you want me to put a bullet into your spine."

Rising, J.C. felt the press of metal into her back.

"The car we're going to take is right over there. I can easily drag you that far."

As they moved forward, Gina went on. "Frankie hot-wired it, so it's all ready for us. It'll take your bodyguards a while to figure out which car is missing and put out the plate number. Wasn't that smart of him? He does have a pretty good idea every once in a while. Get in."

Following Gina's directions, J.C. opened the passenger door and climbed over into the driver's seat. Then Gina said, "Drive."

Stall, she thought. J.C. put the car into Reverse and spent as much time as she dared wiggling it out of the parking space. "What is going on here, Gina?"

"I'm kidnapping you."

"You'll never get away with it. Someone will remember seeing you leave with me." J.C. prayed that was true.

"No matter. I'm being kidnapped, too. That's the beauty of the plan. And when the ransom is paid, I'll be released and you won't."

Yeah, like that's going to work, J.C. thought and tried another tack. "Why are you kidnapping me?"

"For money. Why else?" Gina said. "Turn right at the end of the drive."

Money, the root of all evil, J.C. thought. In the rearview mirror, she caught a glimpse of Nik running around the corner of the house. The Rossis, Theo and Cole Buchanan were right behind him. She managed to flash the emergency lights when she signaled for the right turn.

Nik was coming with the cavalry. She could trust him. Her job now was to distract Gina.

"But aren't you going to get enough money for returning Juliana and Paulo?"

The sound Gina made was nearly a snort. "That was the original plan. And it was supposed to be so easy. All Frankie had to do was go to the church. Gino DeLucca would let him in, he'd get rid of the priest, then he and Gino would kidnap the little bride and groom. Piece of cake. That's what Frankie said. That's what he always says."

J.C. glanced in the rearview mirror. No one was following. "Why did Frankie need the money?"

"Angelo." Gina's tone was bitter. "He's depending on Frankie to come up with at least five million in cash to close that big land deal. It's their only chance to shut the Olivers out. Angelo says that it's time Frankie stepped up to the plate and took some responsibility for the family business. He's always comparing Frankie to Mario Oliver's kids, saying how bright Roman is and how even a girl like Sadie is going to be such an asset to the family. Angelo has never given Frankie the respect he deserves. Helping out with the land deal is Frankie's big chance to prove he can be an asset, too. Otherwise, in a few more years, Angelo will turn everything over to his son Paulo. Frankie and I will be left out in the cold."

"I see," J.C. said. And she thought she was beginning to.

"Angelo thinks Frankie is just a pretty face. No brains. And Frankie does have brains, you know."

Not sure what to say to that, J.C. nodded. "But Frankie didn't have the money to lay out for the land deal?"

"Right. Frankie's got this little weakness for gambling. And then he tried to raise the money by gambling some more."

"And that didn't work," J.C. said, glancing again in the rearview mirror. No Nik.

"If Angelo had just given him more respect and more to do in the business, he wouldn't have had so much free time on his hands."

"So Frankie's in serious debt?"

"Yeah. And Angelo doesn't know anything about Frankie's debts in Las Vegas. He'd have a fit. And the man who lent Frankie money in Vegas—Sammy De-Carlo—he wants his money back. So now poor Frankie has two people pressuring him for cash. Angelo and Sammy."

Poor Frankie? J.C. was hard-pressed not to snort herself. She shot Gina a look and when their eyes met, she was glad she'd stifled it. What she saw confirmed her suspicion that she wasn't just dealing with a dumb blonde. There was anger, irritation and a scary kind of determination in the young woman's eyes.

"What exactly did Frankie say happened at the church?" J.C. slowly eased her foot off the gas pedal and prayed that the traffic light ahead of her would turn red.

"You should know. The plan turned to shit, and Frankie says part of it was your fault. Gino DeLucca was the only person other than Paulo and Juliana and the priest who was supposed to be at that wedding. No one said anything about you being there. And then Roman Oliver shows up and ruins everything. Frankie is in such deep trouble now."

J.C. thought of Roman lying in the hospital about to be arrested for murder and kidnapping, and decided that if there were a continuum for being in "deep trouble," Roman must be pretty close to Frankie along that line.

"Hey!" Gina jabbed the gun into her side. "Put the pedal to the metal and make that light."

J.C. did what she was told. There was a car behind her now, but she was pretty sure it wasn't Nik behind the wheel. Where was he? "But you can still get the ransom money for returning Juliana and Paulo."

Gina made a snort. "That was Plan A. I told you that plan went to shit."

J.C. flicked a glance at Gina, wondering if fear was numbing her brain. "How exactly did it go to shit?"

Gina looked at her as if she were the slow one. "You can't very well collect a ransom if you don't have proof of life. I told Frankie that the FBI always asks for that. So I came up with Plan B. Kidnapping you. This way when the FBI asks for proof that you're alive, we can cut off a finger or a toe and send it to them."

Swallowing hard, J.C. barely missed sideswiping a parked car. Since she didn't like thinking about losing a finger or a toe, she concentrated on the beginning of Gina's explanation. "You don't have proof of life because you've already killed Juliana and Paulo?"

"No. I told you that Frankie's plan went to shit." Gina spoke the words slowly as if she were speaking to a small child. "Frankie never got to do the kidnapping thing, thanks to you and Roman. Frankie was trying to find you when the damn cop arrived, and then he had to make himself scarce. Those two little shits could be honeymooning in Cancún for all I know." Gina's voice was now more shrill than breathy. "Because of you and the cop, they skipped out. I should never have trusted Frankie to handle the plan. There are days when he can't chew gum and walk at the same time, you know? *I* should have hired a stunt double for the charity ball, and then we'd have the money by now. Angelo would be happy. Sammy DeCarlo in Vegas would be happy, and I could have a baby. Frankie promised me a baby when this was all over, and now he's nearly ruined everything."

J.C. sent Gina another assessing look. Part of her mind was focused on what she was going to do to save herself, so maybe that was why she was having trouble following Gina. They were approaching another traffic light, and this time she was going to be more subtle about slowing the car. "Is it really fair to blame Frankie for the screwup? What about the guys he sent up to the choir loft? They screwed up, too, if they let the bride and groom get away."

Gina took her gaze off the road for a minute. "What are you talking about? The only man Frankie had helping him was Gino DeLucca, and Roman Oliver killed him."

"There were at least two other guys at the church. The police arrested them yesterday afternoon."

Gina's eyes narrowed. "You're lying."

Keeping her eyes on the road, J.C. said, "I have no reason to lie. And *someone* sent a ransom note to the two families. Haven't you been watching the news?"

"We've been busy," Gina said. "We had to come up with a new plan. And Frankie was so focused on trying to kill you."

J.C. had half a block to go, and the light ahead of her was amber. This time she was going to stop.

"Dammit, dammit, dammit," Gina fumed. "It's that Roman Oliver. He's got them. Frankie is going to be so upset about this."

"Someone pushed Roman down the stairs. He's in the hospital." J.C. pressed her foot gently on the brake. "Why do you think he's behind the kidnapping?"

"Those other two guys must have been with him. Obviously, they went ahead with the kidnapping plan. If Frankie had just thought of bringing people with him, our plan would have worked. We'd have the money right now."

The light ahead turned yellow. As she braked the car, J.C.'s stomach sank. Gina's explanation sounded way too logical. And then she saw Nik sitting in the car on the side street to her right. If she wasn't mistaken, Theo's car was on the side street to her left. And she was pretty sure that the Rossi brothers were in the car coming toward her. Glancing in the rearview mirror, she saw another car closing the distance behind her. Most likely Cole Buchanan.

They were going to cut her off, she figured. The plan was probably to surround the car and talk Gina into surrendering.

She wasn't sure how Gina would react. The woman wasn't a totally dumb blonde, and she was focused on her mission. She wanted her husband out of trouble, she wanted money and she wanted a baby. J.C. didn't think anyone was going to convince her that she couldn't accomplish her goal.

Heck, Gina might decide to pull the trigger just because Frankie wanted her dead. Dumb or not, Gina was operating on emotion, not rationality. J.C. only had seconds to make her decision.

The light turned red, and J.C. saw Nik start through the intersection. At the last minute, instead of stopping, she floored the gas pedal and jerked the wheel to the left, aiming at the front of the Rossis' car.

"Hey, what are you—"

Satisfied that Gina was momentarily distracted, J.C. lifted one hand off the steering wheel and shoved her gun hand aside. Then her car skidded into Theo's and went into a spin.

This was not part of her plan. J.C. jerked forward and felt the seat belt snap her back. All she'd intended to do was hit Theo's car hard enough to distract Gina and get the gun away. Now she'd lost control. Cole's car grazed her rear bumper and added to the momentum. It was like riding on a very fast merry-go-round. Tires squealed, rubber smoked and Gina screamed. The gun exploded. J.C.'s ears rang with the sound as she jerked forward again. This time pain exploded in her head.

Then everything went black.

WHEN J.C. SURFACED, her mind was a bit fuzzy. But she knew that she was in a hospital room. The IV dripping into her right arm was a dead giveaway. Outside the window, the sky was dark, but there was enough light from a lamp for her to see that her right wrist was in a cast. Not a good sign. She must have been in an accident.

Some of the details flooded back then, the noises, the scents, even the horrible spinning sensation. She kept her eyes open, afraid that if she closed them, she would black out again. To prevent that, she made herself look around the room.

She wasn't alone. A pretty blonde sat in a chair near the window, sewing beads into a piece of silk. Drew Merriweather, the wedding dress designer, she recalled.

Another woman with short dark hair leaned against the doorjamb, her gaze on the TV hanging from the ceiling in the corner. Pepper Rossi, J.C. thought, and on the TV screen, Carla what's-her-name, the Channel Five news reporter, was chattering on about something. The volume was too low to catch much, but the headline beneath the pretty reporter read Kidnapping Plot Foiled.

Suddenly, as if a door had flown open, everything came pouring back into J.C.'s mind. "Nik?" She tried to lever herself up, and winced with pain.

"He's fine." Drew reached her first and laid a hand on her arm that wasn't in a cast. "He's with Kit and Theo and Captain Parker."

Relieved, J.C. turned to Pepper. "Cole and your brothers?"

"They're fine," Pepper assured her. "You were the one who suffered the most damage."

At the question in J.C.'s eyes, she continued, "You have a broken wrist and a mild concussion." She paused to grin down at her. "You look like hell, but you took that crazy blonde down."

"Is she…?" J.C. winced as she searched her mind for more details. The gun had gone off. That much she remembered very clearly.

"Don't worry," Pepper said. "Gina Carlucci has a black eye, nothing serious enough to keep her from singing her lungs out to everyone who'll listen. Frankie Carlucci has lawyered up, but according to Cole, Gina is willing to serve him up on a silver platter."

"I guess she's decided to cut her losses," J.C. said. "She claimed that all she wanted out of this was a baby."

Drew and Pepper stared at her.

"I know," she said. "It's just not pretty when you consider what she and Frankie might have produced in the way of offspring." Another thought occurred to her. "I need to talk to Nik. Frankie hired a stunt double to take his place at the charity ball. I know the name of the company that he probably used."

"Relax." Drew patted her hand. "There'll be time enough for that."

"Gina's probably already given the police that information, anyway," Pepper said. "We're supposed to see that you don't get upset and that you rest." She wrinkled her nose. "While the men do manly stuff."

J.C. frowned, but when the pain on her forehead blossomed, she thought better of it. "Gina swears that she and Frankie didn't kidnap Paulo and Juliana and that they didn't send the ransom notes. She's convinced that Roman is behind the kidnapping because he ruined their plan." One look at Pepper's and Drew's faces confirmed her fear. "That's what Nik and Kit and Theo are talking to Captain Parker about, isn't it? They're still going to arrest Roman, aren't they?"

Before either of the other women could answer, there was a knock on the door, and J.C. noted that Pepper drew a gun. "Who is it?"

"Sam Schaeffer," said a voice on the other side of the door.

Tucking her gun back in her jacket pocket, Pepper opened the door, and Sam entered.

He glanced quickly around. "I'm sorry. I know I'm intruding. I just need a minute."

"What is it?" J.C. asked. Sam looked about as bad as she felt. His face was pale, and there were circles under his eyes. In the lamplight, she suddenly noticed how fragile the young man looked. "Sit down," she urged.

Pepper immediately nudged Sam toward the chair that Drew had vacated earlier.

"I won't stay long," he said.

"You're upset. Why don't you tell us what happened?" Drew asked.

"Captain Parker is taking Roman's statement. And then they're going to arrest him. I thought…I was so sure that Frankie and Gina Carlucci were behind everything."

"And they're not," J.C. said.

"No. Something more is going on here. And Roman is not involved. We just have to find out who is."

Later, J.C. wondered how she had seen it. But there was something about the way Sam's voice broke that had a series of images flashing through her mind. The way he'd dropped his notebook in Parker's office the day before, the way he'd laughed at her remark about the movie *Fargo*. And now…he was so upset about Roman's arrest. Would a young man who was Theo's intern be that upset? Unless… If she'd been Nik, she bet her thumbs would have been pricking.

"You're Sadie Oliver, aren't you?" she asked.

Immediately, Sam—Sadie—tensed and her already pale face turned even whiter. "Please. Don't turn me in. I'm not asking for myself, but I can't let Theo's career suffer because of this."

"Why would it?" Drew asked.

"Because he's known all along who I am. He's lied to everyone. And I'm wanted by the police. They'll arrest him for aiding and abetting a fugitive. I can't let that happen." She met each one of the women's eyes in turn. "I won't let that happen. I promise that I'll turn myself in. It would just be better for Theo if I changed back into my own clothes first. Then no one needs to know that I've been masquerading as his intern."

Sitting down on the arm of the chair, Drew put a hand on Sadie's shoulder. "We're not going to turn you in. And if you're thinking of doing that yourself, I can tell you that I've been there and tried that. If Theo decides that you shouldn't turn yourself in, well…"

Out of deference to the stitches on her forehead, J.C. decided to forgo a nod. "These Angelis men have a way of getting their own way."

"You know, I sometimes have the same trouble with Cole," Pepper said. "At least I let him think I do."

The four women exchanged glances and even Sadie's lips twitched in a smile.

"Why don't you tell us what really happened at the church," J.C. said.

Sadie met her eyes. "I'm touched that you would trust me to do that."

"Kit would trust Roman with his life," Drew said.

"We know that the two of you couldn't be involved in kidnapping your sister and Paulo Carlucci," J.C. added.

Sadie folded her hands together in her lap. "I got there late. If I'd just gotten there on time, I might have been able to…" When her voice broke, she swallowed and drew in a deep breath. "I talked to Roman yesterday. Theo arranged for me to get in. I suspected that my father was pressuring the doctors to stall for more time before they would approve a visit by the police. And I was right. But when I talked to Roman, he couldn't tell me much more than we already know. Except that he received the same note from Juliana that I did. It was delivered that afternoon around four, inviting us to come to the church. We didn't know we were being invited to a wedding. And we're pretty sure Juliana didn't send them.

"When I got to St. Peter's, I heard two shots. Then a man with a gun burst through the vestibule doors and ran up the stairs to the choir loft. Roman was right on his heels, and he shoved me under the staircase. There was a shot from the loft and Roman raced up the stairs."

"That must have been the shot I fired," Drew said. "I hit that man in the shoulder. Roman told us to run. Then the man attacked Roman."

"I was standing there under the stairs when Roman fell. I called 911 and then the man with the gun came down the stairs and ran out the front door. Roman told me to call Kit and I tried, but the answering machine picked up."

"Paulo and Juliana and I ran along the side of the choir loft and out the back door," Drew said. "We were about two blocks away when Paulo put me in a taxi."

"I saw that from the window in the choir loft," Sadie said. "I also saw a dark-colored van I'd seen earlier following Paulo and Juliana. I took the same route out of the church, but when I reached the corner, they'd disappeared."

When she paused, Drew gave her a glass of water. After taking a swallow, Sadie went on. "I suppose I panicked. I've practiced enough law to know that this wasn't going to look good for Roman and that I wasn't going to do him any good by hanging around. The police were there. So I got in my car and followed the ambulance to the hospital. I tried again to reach Kit at his home phone, and his aunt Cass told me Kit was at the fishing cabin. That's where I found Theo. I convinced him not to turn me in and to let me help him work on the case."

"I think that was a good plan," J.C. said. "In your shoes, I would have done the same thing."

"Me, too," Drew said.

"I'll make that unanimous," Pepper added. "I made a similar deal with Cole when we were tracking down a stolen painting."

Sadie took another sip of water, then said, "If I'd only gotten to the church sooner—"

"You might have been killed," J.C. said. "Sometimes the Fates weave everything together just perfectly."

18

"WE'RE NOT MAKING any progress. It's been two days, and the noose around Roman's neck just keeps getting tighter." Kit tried to pace off his frustration on the landing of the stairwell. Theo lounged against the wall while Nik kept his weight pressed firmly against the open door so that he had a view of the hospital corridor and the entrance to J.C.'s room. He'd wanted to be with J.C., but he'd had to be there for Roman and Mario Oliver when Captain Parker had made the arrest. And he had to be with his brothers now because Kit's temper was on a short leash.

"Gina Carlucci could be lying," Kit said.

"I don't think so." Theo sighed. "I watched part of the interrogation before Parker and I came over here. She's spilling everything in the hopes that she'll get leniency. If she and Frankie had kidnapped those kids, she'd be giving them up, too."

Kit made a grunting noise and continued to pace. "That still doesn't mean that Roman is behind it."

Theo said nothing and Nik shifted his gaze to his brothers. He'd urged them onto the landing in the stairwell because the waiting room was pretty full, and he knew that Kit was ready to blow. When his youngest brother had heard about Frankie and Gina's arrest, he'd been so certain that Roman would be cleared.

Hell, Nik thought, he'd been certain, too. He glanced back down the corridor. When Mario Oliver had learned that J.C. was in the emergency room and that the doctors had wanted her to stay overnight, he'd arranged to have her brought up to a private room down the hall from Roman's.

When you donated a trauma center to a hospital, Nik guessed you had the power to make those kinds of arrangements. And he was grateful to Mario.

She'd looked so fragile when the EMTs had loaded her onto the gurney at the accident scene. And there'd been so much blood on her face. They'd told him not to worry, that the blood was from her nose and the cut on her forehead, and that she hadn't been seriously hurt. But he couldn't seem to erase from his mind those final images when she'd shot her car into the intersection.

For the third time in two days, he'd almost lost her.

For a moment, his thoughts were interrupted when he saw Philly step out of the elevator with a bouquet of daffodils in her hand. His first thought was that she'd somehow learned of J.C.'s accident, perhaps from Aunt Cass. But she didn't go to J.C.'s room. She went straight to Roman's.

Sweet, he thought. Roman had saved her life, so the two were connected in a way. The moment that Philly disappeared from view, he turned his attention back to J.C.'s door. A few minutes ago, Mayor and Mrs. Riley had visited J.C., but they hadn't stayed long, and now Drew, Pepper and Sam Schaeffer were back with her.

"She should be getting some rest," Nik remarked.

His brothers both turned to look at him.

"You're worried about Gina Carlucci getting rest?" Theo asked.

"No, of course not."

"That's who we were talking about," Theo explained.

Nik frowned at him. "I'm worried about J.C."

As his brothers continued to study him, Nik saw understanding in Kit's eyes and speculation in Theo's.

"So that's how it is," Theo finally murmured.

"What's that supposed to mean?" Nik asked.

Theo's glance flicked to Kit and then back to Nik. "It would seem that Cupid has been busy this weekend."

"Is anyone here besides me worried about Roman?" Kit questioned sharply.

"We're going to find the answers."

The certainty in Theo's tone had both Kit and Nik glancing at him.

"Are you saying that because you feel it?" Kit asked. "Or are you speaking as his defense attorney?"

Though neither of them would admit it to his face, both Nik and Kit had always known that the psychic sense Theo possessed was stronger than theirs. He'd inherited more than his looks from their mother.

"I'm speaking from my experience as your brother. Watching Parker charge Roman Oliver with kidnapping and murder was bad. But you're both going to bounce back from it. And then we're going to figure out who's really behind all this."

"Cole and the Rossis are already trying to figure out the cash angle. If we can rely on Gina's understanding,

Angelo Carlucci stands to lose out on the land deal now that Frankie can't ante up the cash," Nik said. "He's a smart man. Maybe he never depended on Frankie at all. If the news of the secret wedding was leaked to Frankie, could be Angelo got wind of it, too, learned about Frankie's plans and decided to make some of his own."

"Not a bad theory," Theo said. "But we shouldn't eliminate the Oliver camp from suspicion."

"Roman is not guilty." Kit made a move toward Theo, but Nik was faster. He inserted himself in between them and pressed both hands against Kit's shoulders.

"Not here, Kit," Nik said. "And he's not talking about Roman."

Kit backed away. Nik followed him a few steps, but he remained between his two brothers. Theo's temper took longer to ignite, but it was there.

"Everyone needed cash for this deal." Theo lifted both hands, palms up and then lowered one. "If you take the money from the other family, you gain what might be a decisive advantage in the negotiations."

"He has a point, Kit," Nik said.

"If we're going to start picking suspects from the Olivers' camp, then my money's on Sadie," Kit said.

"Sadie's not behind this."

The flatness in Theo's tone had both his brothers staring at him again. Suddenly, several things began to slip into place in Nik's mind.

"She was at the church and she left," Kit pointed out. "Her prints are on the ransom note along with Roman's. And she took off. If she's so innocent, why hasn't she shown up?"

"Because then she'd be under arrest just as Roman's under arrest," Theo said. For the first time, the anger and frustration they were all feeling could be heard in Theo's tone. "Roman says he got a note from Juliana inviting him to the church. Perhaps Sadie got one, too. What if the plan was to set them up as the fall guys?"

"You mean frame them for the kidnapping?" Kit asked.

"That would explain why the kidnap notes had their fingerprints on them," Nik said. "You think someone was out to frame them."

"Or lure them there to kill them. They very nearly succeeded with Roman," Theo said. "It was very carefully planned. If Frankie Carlucci and Gino DeLucca hadn't had their own kidnapping plan, it might have worked."

Kit moved again, and this time Nik shoved him against the wall.

"Dammit, he knows something that we don't," Kit said.

"Yeah." Keeping a firm grip on Kit, Nik turned to face Theo. "He does know something. Why don't you tell us who your intern, Sam Schaeffer, really is, bro?"

IT TOOK ANOTHER fifteen minutes or so to get his brothers sorted out. Then Drew left with Kit, and Theo picked up Sadie. Nik wanted to thank Mario Oliver for making arrangements for J.C., but when he glanced in Roman's room, he saw that Philly was still there. One of her hands was in Mario's and the other was resting on one of Roman's. She was comforting both of them, he thought, so he didn't interrupt. Instead, he conveyed his thanks to Michael Dano, the man who seemed to be Mario

Oliver's right hand in the absence of his son and daughters.

Finally, he let himself into J.C.'s room. Theo had advised him to pick up some flowers in the gift shop. All they'd had were some daffodils, which were still buds. The woman at the cash register had assured him that they'd bloom just as soon as they warmed up a bit, and then she'd talked him into buying some chocolate, but it wasn't Ghirardelli's.

The moment Nik entered, Pepper Rossi rose from the lone chair in the room. "Looks like this is my cue to leave."

And she did. He'd already told Cole that they could both go home, that he intended to stay the night with J.C. No one thought that she was really in any mortal danger now that Frankie and Gina were behind bars. But he wasn't taking any chances.

The nerves that had been knotting in his stomach ever since he'd sent his brothers on their way tightened.

"Hi," she said.

Her face was so pale, almost as white as the bandage they'd used to cover the stitches on her forehead. He couldn't prevent the last few seconds before the crash from flooding his mind, her car shooting forward. He'd slammed on his brakes, but not in time to keep from hitting her. Then there'd been the sound of metal crashing into metal, the squeal of tires, the smell of burning rubber, the shattering of glass. And when he'd managed to get free of his own car and get to her, there'd been so much blood.

Suddenly the nerves in his stomach coalesced into anger. "What the hell did you think you were doing?"

J.C. STARED AT HIM. A moment ago he'd looked so sweet standing there with daffodils in one hand and a box of candy in the other. Now he was furious with her.

"What are you talking about?"

"I had a plan. We were going to surround your car and talk her out of it." He stalked across the room and tossed the flowers and chocolates down on the bed. "You didn't have to end up this way."

J.C. levered herself up on her good arm. "We're talking Gina Carlucci here. Her elevator does not go to the top floor. Believe me, your chances of talking her out of shooting me were at best fifty-fifty. And I didn't like the odds."

"You could have been killed." He nearly snarled the words. "I love you and you could have been killed."

"Well, here's a bulletin—I wasn't killed. And I love you, too!"

For a moment, neither one of them spoke. The snarled and shouted words hung in the silence that suddenly filled the room.

Nik sat down on the side of her bed as if his legs had suddenly gone weak. J.C. was glad that she was already lying down.

His eyes hadn't left hers. She could see the anger, and something else, too.

He swallowed hard, then said, "Do you mean it? Do you love me?"

"No. I just said it to make you crazy." She paused long enough to swallow. "Of course, I mean it. Did you mean it?"

He glanced down at the bed and then smiled at her. "Yeah. I've never thrown flowers and candy at any other woman. So it must be love." He reached for the fingers of her good hand and raised them to his lips. She felt her pulse scramble.

"I guess this will shoot the whole sex-buddy thing out the window?" He turned her hand over and scraped his teeth lightly over her wrist.

J.C. shivered. "I guess."

"Too bad," he murmured. "I really liked being your sex buddy."

Her heart was pounding fast now, but she managed to smile. "Maybe we could work something out."

He leaned closer and pressed his mouth against hers. She was just sinking into the kiss when he drew back, swearing under his breath.

"What? Have you changed your mind? Are you going to take it all back?" she asked.

"No." He nearly frowned at her. "Since I blew the flowers-and-candy thing, I have another present for you." After placing her hand carefully back on the sheet, he reached into his pocket, and pulled out a small blue box.

She simply stared at it. When he opened it, she continued to stare—at the ring. Nerves twisted in his stomach. Obviously, she was speechless. And it took a lot to make J.C. Riley speechless. At least he hoped that was the reason for the dumbfounded look on her face.

Clearing his throat, he said, "I know it's probably rushing things. But we haven't really done any of this slowly. I think I fell in love with you when you stepped out of that closet."

She met his eyes then, and what he saw in them made him forget the rest of what he wanted to say.

"Where did you get it? When did you get it? Aren't

you going to put it on me?" She held out her good hand. "They don't sell these in the hospital gift shop."

She was talking again. That was a good sign. Nik slipped it on her finger. Perfect fit.

When he leaned in to kiss her again, she put a hand on his chest, and he answered one of the questions in her eyes. "I called the personal shopper at the St. Regis. She messengered it over." He shrugged. "You mentioned we needed a diamond."

"Yes, I did. And obviously, I'm the boss." Laughing, J.C. linked the fingers of her good hand with his. "You haven't asked me yet."

Nik grinned at her. "The ring's on you, Jude Catherine. From this moment, you're mine."

"And you're mine."

"Okay. Now about this sex-buddy thing." He eased her back onto the pillow, and made room for himself beside her. "I have a plan. Let me show you."

And he did.

* * * * *

Wait!
The excitement's not over yet!!!

Theo Angelis still has an adventure—and
a very sexy woman—waiting for him.
And he's not prepared for either one of them....

Don't miss
THE DEFENDER,
available next month.

Here's a sneak peak....

THEO FLOATED ON HIS BACK in the water, enjoying the gentle movement of the waves. Above him the moon and stars crowded the clear night sky. He'd lost track of the number of laps he'd swum, but even though his muscles were weak, his mind relaxed, he hadn't been able to get Sadie Oliver out of his mind. Sooner or later, he was going to have to figure out why.

He was about to climb onto the dock when the silence was broken by a sharp, staccato knocking sound. Then he heard Bob hit the screen door. Grabbing the dock with one hand, Theo glanced toward the shore. He couldn't imagine either Kit or Nik knocking on the cabin door. From the angle he was at a tree blocked his view, but he clearly heard Bob bark and launch himself at the door again.

Bob was not the best watchdog. In spite of his size, the dog had the people-loving instincts of a golden retriever and viewed any stranger as a possible source of petting or food and hopefully both.

Staying very still in the water, Theo waited and a moment later saw a figure move around the side of the cabin. He got a quick impression of height—the build was more slender than either of his brothers. He'd left the light on in his bedroom, and when the figure turned to face the window, he had a clear view of a silhouette in profile. Female, he thought. The light wasn't strong enough for him to see her features, but he made out that she was wearing a skirt.

Annoyance and frustration streamed through him. Following the arrest of his stalker, he'd convinced the group of women who'd been attending his trials for the past few months to stop. And they had. For the last two months, he'd thought that he'd gotten his life back to normal.

But he couldn't think of another reason why a woman would have come all this way to track him down at midnight. He wasn't dating anyone. And this woman was too tall to be his sister Philly. Besides, Philly would have walked right in. She and Bob were old friends.

The figure moved back toward the front of the cabin, her knock louder this time. He thought of calling out to her, but didn't. Instead, moving quietly, he swam toward shore, and once he got his feet beneath him, he walked slowly out of the water. He was still twenty yards away when he saw her open the screen door and walk in. He had to give her points for courage. Bob might be a pushover, but he did have that size thing going for him. To his surprise, he saw her crouch down and speak to the dog, but the sound of the waves behind him muffled her words. Okay, so she had guts and she liked big dogs. But she was still in a place she had no business being. Technically, she was breaking and entering.

She'd already disappeared into the cabin by the time he reached it. Carefully, he opened the porch door and turned sideways to slip in before the hinge creaked.

She'd left the inner door to the cabin open. In the darkness of the kitchen, he could only make out her silhouette as she stood peering out the window in the direction of the lake.

Annoyance streamed through him again. Bold as brass, he thought. Not only had she followed him out here to a place that he'd always considered a refuge, but she'd walked right in. It didn't help his mood one bit that Bob was sitting at her feet, beating his tail against the floor, evidently pleased as punch at the new visitor. At the very least, Theo figured he owed her a good scare.

He flipped on the light. "What the hell do you think—"

She wirled and her scream blocked the rest of his sentence.

"Sadie?" Since he hadn't been able to get her out of his mind while he was swimming, his first thought was that he'd conjured her up. His second was that in another moment she was going to slip right to the floor. Cursing himself, he strode to her. She'd gone pale as the moonlight on the water. "Are you all right?"

Stupid question when he could see that she was anything but. Taking her arm, he eased her into one of the chairs at the table. Then he moved to the refrigerator, retrieved the bottle of wine he'd opened earlier and filled a glass. She was still trembling when he set it in front of her, so he took the chair next to hers and covered her hand with his to help her lift the glass.

She took a sip and swallowed. Then their eyes met and held over the rim of the glass. He was touching only her hand, and yet there was that intensity, that same connection he'd felt when he'd clasped her hand in the courtroom. Suddenly, Theo knew. Not merely that their paths would cross again, but that she was the *one,* the one woman for him.

No. Panic shot up his spine, and nerves knotted in his abdomen. He wasn't ready. He forced himself to take a deep breath as he reminded himself that he still had a choice. The Fates only presented choices.

But as Sadie lifted the glass for another sip, he didn't remove his hand from hers, and he couldn't seem to take his eyes off her. Her lips were parted and moist from the wine. He very badly wanted to taste that mouth. Even as lust curled into a tight hot fist in his stomach, he let his hand drop and eased himself back in his chair. He had to get away before…

Rising, he strode toward the adjoining hallway. "Drink the wine while I change. then you can tell me why you're here."

SADIE LET OUT THE BREATH she hadn't even been aware she was holding and barely kept the wineglass from slipping out of her hand. Very carefully, she set it on the table. Her head was still foggy, still spinning. And it wasn't merely because he'd scared her. It was because he'd touched her again. All he'd meant to do was steady the wineglass, just as all he'd done in that courtroom was shake her hand.

How was it that each time he put a hand on her, even in the most casual of ways, it was as if he'd touched her all over?

She pressed her fingers to her temples, willing her mind to clear and her thoughts to settle. When she'd whirled to see him standing in the doorway, he hadn't looked like the Theo Angelis she'd seen in court. He'd looked larger than life, like some god from the sea, his dark hair slicked back, those even darker eyes with that hint of danger. And all that damp, tanned skin. Even now, she was astonished at how much she wanted to touch him, to taste him. More than that, she wanted to devour him.

No man had ever affected her this way. With hands that trembled, she reached for her wine and took another swallow.

She was overreacting. There were too many emotions pounding at her—Roman, Juliana, the walk through the woods. She had to get a grip. She'd come here to ask Kit Angelis to help her. She couldn't afford to fall apart.

"I'm sorry I gave you a scare."

Startled, she whirled in her chair to watch Theo pour himself a glass of wine. Then he reached into the refrigerator and pulled out a plate of cheese. He was wearing old jeans that had faded at the seams and hem and an equally ancient T-shirt. The general rattiness of the clothes surprised her. Theo had always been so impeccably dressed in his court appearances.

"These are my lucky fishing clothes."

Sadie's gaze flew to his face. Could he read her mind? Was she that transparent to him?

His lips curved as he set the plate of cheese between them and sank into a chair. "Whenever I wear them, I catch the biggest fish. My brothers are hoping that one day soon the cloth will disintegrate and fall off me."

In her mind, Sadie pictured them doing just that— first the T-shirt, the jeans... Was he wearing briefs beneath them? As heat pooled in her center, Sadie ruthlessly focused. She was not going to get anywhere if she continued to imagine Theo Angelis naked.

* * * * *

Every Life Has More Than One Chapter

Award-winning author Stevi Mittman delivers another hysterical mystery, featuring Teddi Bayer, an irrepressible heroine, and her to-die-for hero, Detective Drew Scoones. After all, life on Long Island can be murder!

Turn the page for a sneak peek
at the warm and funny fourth book,
WHOSE NUMBER IS UP, ANYWAY?,
in the Teddi Bayer series,
by STEVI MITTMAN.
On sale August 7

"Before redecorating a room, I always advise my clients to empty it of everything but one chair. Then I suggest they move that chair from place to place, sitting in it, until the placement feels right. Trust your instincts when deciding on furniture placement. Your room should "feel right.""
—TipsFromTeddi.com

Gut feelings. You know, that gnawing in the pit of your stomach that warns you that you are about to do the absolute stupidest thing you could do? Something that will ruin life as you know it?

I've got one now, standing at the butcher counter in King Kullen, the grocery store in the same strip mall as L.I. Lanes, the bowling alley cum billiard parlor I'm in the process of redecorating for its "Grand Opening."

I realize being in the wrong supermarket probably doesn't sound exactly dire to you, but you aren't the one buying your father a brisket at a store your mother will somehow know isn't Waldbaum's.

And then, June Bayer isn't your mother.

The woman behind the counter has agreed to go into the freezer to find a brisket for me, since there aren't any in the case. There are packages of pork tenderloin, piles of spare ribs and rolls of sausage, but no briskets.

Warning Number Two, right? I should be so out of here.

But no, I'm still in the same spot when she comes back out, brisketless, her face ashen. She opens her mouth as if she is going to scream, but only a gurgle comes out.

And then she pinballs out from behind the counter, knocking bottles of Peter Luger Steak Sauce to the floor on her way, now hitting the tower of cans at the end of the prepared foods aisle and sending them sprawling, now making her way down the aisle, careening from side to side as she goes.

Finally, from a distance, I hear her shout, "He's deeeeeeaaaad! Joey's deeeeeaaaad."

My first thought is *You should always trust your gut.*

My second thought is that now, somehow, my mother will know I was in King Kullen. For weeks I will have to hear "What did you expect?" as though whenever you go to King Kullen someone turns up dead. And if the detective investigating the case turns out to be Detective Drew Scoones…well, I'll never hear the end of that from her, either.

She still suspects I murdered the guy who was found dead on my doorstep last Halloween just to get Drew back into my life.

Several people head for the butcher's freezer and I position myself to block them. If there's one thing I've learned from finding people dead—and the guy on my doorstep wasn't the first one—it's that the police get very testy when you mess with their murder scenes.

"You can't go in there until the police get here," I say,

stationing myself at the end of the butcher's counter and in front of the Employees Only door, acting as if I'm some sort of authority. "You'll contaminate the evidence if it turns out to be murder."

Shouts and chaos. You'd think I'd know better than to throw the word *murder* around. Cell phones are flipping open and tongues are wagging.

I amend my statement quickly. "Which, of course, it probably isn't. Murder, I mean. People die all the time, and it's not always in hospitals or their own beds, or…" I babble when I'm nervous, and the idea of someone dead on the other side of the freezer door makes me very nervous.

So does the idea of seeing Drew Scoones again. Drew and I have this on-again, off-again sort of thing…that I kind of turned off.

Who knew he'd take it so personally when he tried to get serious and I responded by saying we could talk about *us* tomorrow—and then caught a plane to my parents' condo in Boca the next day? In July. In the middle of a job.

For some crazy reason, he took that to mean that I was avoiding him and the subject of *us*.

That was three months ago. I haven't seen him since.

The manager, who identifies himself and points to his nameplate in case I don't believe him, says he has to go into *his cooler*. "Maybe Joey's not dead," he says. "Maybe he can be saved, and you're letting him die in there. Did you ever think of that?"

In fact, I hadn't. But I had thought that the murderer might try to go back in to make sure his tracks were covered, so I say that I will go in and check.

Which means that the manager and I couple up and go in together while everyone pushes against the doorway to peer in, erasing any chance of finding clean prints on that Employee Only door.

I expect to find carcasses of dead animals hanging from hooks, and maybe Joey hanging from one, too. I think it's going to be very creepy and I steel myself, only to find a rather benign series of shelves with large slabs of meat laid out carefully on them, along with boxes and boxes marked simply Chicken.

Nothing scary here, unless you count the body of a middle-aged man with graying hair sprawled faceup on the floor. His eyes are wide open and unblinking. His shirt is stiff. His pants are stiff. His body is stiff. And his expression, you should forgive the pun—is frozen. Bill-the-manager crosses himself and stands mute while I pronounce the guy dead in a sort of *happy now?* tone.

"We should not be in here," I say, and he nods his head emphatically and helps me push people out of the doorway just in time to hear the police sirens and see the cop cars pull up outside the big store windows.

Bobbie Lyons, my partner in Teddi Bayer Interior Designs (and also my neighbor, my best friend and my private fashion police), and Mark, our carpenter (and my dogsitter, confidant, and ego booster), rush in from next door. They beat the cops by a half step and shout out my name. People point in my direction.

After all the publicity that followed the unfortunate incident during which I shot my ex-husband, Rio Gallo, and then the subsequent murder of my first client— which I solved, I might add—it seems like the whole world, or at least all of Long Island, knows who I am.

Mark asks if I'm all right. (Did I remember to mention that the man is drop-dead-gorgeous-but-a-decade-too-young-for-me-yet-too-old-for-my-daughter-thank-god?) I don't get a chance to answer him because the police are quickly closing in on the store manager and me.

"The woman—" I begin telling the police. Then I have to pause for the manager to fill in her name, which he does: *Fran*.

I continue. "Right. Fran. Fran went into the freezer to get a brisket. A moment later she came out and screamed that Joey was dead. So I'd say she was the one who discovered the body."

"And you are…?" the cop asks me. It comes out a bit like who do I *think* I am, rather than who am I really?

"An innocent bystander," Bobbie, hair perfect, makeup just right, says, carefully placing her body between the cop and me.

"And she was just leaving," Mark adds. They each take one of my arms.

Fran comes into the inner circle surrounding the cops. In case it isn't obvious from the hairnet and blood-stained white apron with Fran embroidered on it, I explain that she was the butcher who was going for the brisket. Mark and Bobbie take that as a signal that I've done my job and they can now get me out of there. They twist around, with me in the middle, as if we're a Rock-ettes line, until we are facing away from the butcher counter. They've managed to propel me a few steps toward the exit when disaster—in the form of a Mazda RX7 pulling up at the loading curb—strikes.

Mark's grip on my arm tightens like a vise. "Too late," he says.

Bobbie's expletive is unprintable. "Maybe there's a back door," she suggests, but Mark is right. It's too late.

I've laid my eyes on Detective Scoones. And while my gut is trying to warn me that my heart shouldn't go there, regions farther south are melting at just the sight of him.

"Walk," Bobbie orders me.

And I try to. Really.

Walk, I tell my feet. *Just put one foot in front of the other.*

I can do this because I know, in my heart of hearts, that if Drew Scoones was still interested in me, he'd have gotten in touch with me after I returned from Boca. And he didn't.

Since he's a detective, Drew doesn't have to wear one of those dark blue Nassau County Police uniforms. Instead, he's got on jeans, a tight-fitting T-shirt and a tweedy sports jacket. If you think that sounds good, you should see him. Chiseled features, cleft chin, brown hair that's naturally a little sandy in the front, a smile that…well, that doesn't matter. He isn't smiling now.

He walks up to me, tucks his sunglasses into his breast pocket and looks me over from head to toe.

"Well, if it isn't Miss Cut and Run," he says. "Aren't you supposed to be somewhere in Florida or something?" He looks at Mark accusingly, as if he was covering for me when he told Drew I was gone.

"Detective Scoones?" one of the uniforms says. "The stiff's in the cooler and the woman who found him is over there." He jerks his head in Fran's direction.

Drew continues to stare at me.

You know how when you were young, your mother always told you to wear clean underwear in case you were in an accident? And how, a little farther on, she told you not to go out in hair rollers because you never knew who you might see—or who might see you? And how now your best friend says she wouldn't be caught dead without makeup and suggests you shouldn't either?

Okay, today, *finally*, in my overalls and Converse sneakers, I get it.

I brush my hair out of my eyes. "Well, I'm back," I say. As if he hasn't known my exact whereabouts. The man is a detective, for heaven's sake. "Been back awhile."

Bobbie has watched the exchange and apparently decided she's given Drew all the time he deserves. "And we've got work to do, so…" she says, grabbing my arm and giving Drew a little two-fingered wave goodbye.

As I back up a foot or two, the store manager sees his chance and places himself in front of Drew, trying to get his attention. Maybe what makes Drew such a good detective is his ability to focus.

Only what he's focusing on is me.

"Phone broken? Carrier pigeon died?" he asks me, taking in Fran, the manager, the meat counter and that Employees Only door, all without taking his eyes off me.

Mark tries to break the spell. "We've got work to do there, you've got work to do here, Scoones," Mark says to him, gesturing toward next door. "So it's back to the alley for us."

Drew's lip twitches. "You working the alley now?" he says.

"If you'd like to follow me," Bill-the-manager, clearly exasperated, says to Drew—who doesn't respond. It's as if waiting for my answer is all he has to do.

So, fine. "You knew I was back," I say.

The man has known my whereabouts every hour of the day for as long as I've known him. And my mother's not the only one who won't buy that he "just happened" to answer this particular call. In fact, I'm willing to bet my children's lunch money that he's taken every call within ten miles of my home since the day I got back.

And now he's gotten lucky.

"*You* could have called *me*," I say.

"You're the one who said *tomorrow* for our talk and then flew the coop, chickie," he says. "I figured the ball was in your court."

"Detective?" the uniform says. "There's something you ought to see in here."

Drew gives me a look that amounts to *in or out?*

He could be talking about the investigation, or about our relationship.

Bobbie tries to steer me away. Mark's fists are balled. Drew waits me out, knowing I won't be able to resist what might be a murder investigation.

Finally he turns and heads for the cooler.

And, like a puppy dog, I follow.

Bobbie grabs the back of my shirt and pulls me to a halt.

"I'm just going to show him something," I say, yanking away.

"Yeah," Bobbie says, pointedly looking at the buttons on my blouse. The two at breast level have popped. "That's what I'm afraid of."

HARLEQUIN®

Mediterranean NIGHTS™

*Glamour, elegance, mystery and revenge
aboard the high seas...*

Coming in August 2007...

THE TYCOON'S SON

by
award-winning author

Cindy Kirk

Businessman Theo Catomeris's long-estranged father is determined to reconnect with his son, so he hires Trish Melrose to persuade Theo to renew his contract with Liberty Line. Sailing aboard the luxurious *Alexandra's Dream* is a rare opportunity for the single mom to mix business and pleasure. But an undeniable attraction between Trish and Theo is distracting her from the task at hand....

HM38967

REQUEST YOUR FREE BOOKS!

2 FREE NOVELS PLUS 2 FREE GIFTS!

HARLEQUIN®

Blaze®

Red-hot reads!

HARLEQUIN®

Super Romance®

*Looking for a romantic, emotional
and unforgettable escape?*

*You'll find it this month and every month
with a Harlequin Superromance!*

Rory Gorenzi has a sense of humor and a sense of
honor. She also happens to be good with children.

Seamus Lee, widower and father of four, needs
someone with exactly those traits.

They meet at the Colorado mountain school owned
by Rory's father, where she teaches skiing and
avalanche safety. But Seamus—and his children—
learn more from her than that....

Look for

GOOD WITH CHILDREN

by Margot Early,

*available August 2007, and these other
fantastic titles from Harlequin Superromance.*

Silhouette® Desire

REASONS FOR REVENGE

A brand-new provocative miniseries by *USA TODAY*
bestselling author **Maureen Child** begins with

SCORNED BY THE BOSS

Jefferson Lyon is a man used to having his own way.
He runs his shipping empire from California, and
his admin Caitlyn Monroe runs the rest of his world.
When Caitlin decides she's had enough and needs
new scenery, Jefferson devises a plan to get her back.
Jefferson *never* loses, but little does he know that
he's in a competition....

Don't miss any of the other titles from the
REASONS FOR REVENGE trilogy by
USA TODAY bestselling author **Maureen Child.**

SCORNED BY THE BOSS #1816
Available August 2007

SEDUCED BY THE RICH MAN #1820
Available September 2007

CAPTURED BY THE BILLIONAIRE #1826
Available October 2007

Only from Silhouette Desire!

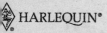
HARLEQUIN®

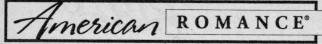
American | ROMANCE®

TEXAS LEGACIES: THE CARRIGANS

Get to the Heart of a Texas Family

WITH

THE RANCHER NEXT DOOR
by
Cathy Gillen Thacker

She'll Run The Ranch—And Her Life—Her Way!

On her alpaca ranch in Texas, Rebecca encounters
constant interference from Trevor McCabe, the
bossy rancher next door. Rebecca becomes very
friendly with Vince Owen, her other neighbor and
Trevor's archrival from college. Trevor's problem
is convincing Rebecca that he is on her side, and
aware of Vince's ulterior motives. But Trevor has
fallen for her in the process....

On sale July 2007

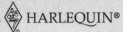

HARLEQUIN®

Blaze™

COMING NEXT MONTH

#339 HARD AND FAST Lisa Renee Jones
She's been in and out of locker rooms her whole life. Now Amanda Wright is there looking for the inside scoop to take her column to the big leagues. When pitcher Brad Rogers offers a sexy time in exchange for an interview, her libido won't let her refuse!

#340 DOING IRELAND! Kate Hoffmann
Lust in Translation
A spring that inspires instant lust? With the way her life's been going, Claire O'Connor is ready to try anything—even if it means boarding a plane to Ireland. But once she arrives, she knows there has to be *something* to the legend. Because all she had to do was set eyes on gorgeous innkeeper Will Donovan, and she wanted him….

#341 STRIPPED Julie Elizabeth Leto
The Bad Girls Club, Bk. 2
Lilith St. John is a witch—really! And she hasn't been too good lately. (It seems using a spell to make Mac Mancusi totally infatuated with her was a big no-no. Who knew?) But that doesn't mean she deserves to be stripped of her powers. Especially now—when Mac's suddenly back in her life, looking to rekindle the magic…

#342 THE DEFENDER Cara Summers
Tall, Dark…and Dangerously Hot! Bk. 3
Theo Angelis puts the "hot" in "hotshot lawyer," but savvy, sexy Sadie Oliver's simple handshake sets him aflame. Her brother's facing a murder rap, their sister is missing and Sadie is in terrible danger. Her only way to be involved in the case is to pose as a man. But the heat in Theo's eyes never lets her forget she's *all* woman....

#343 PICK ME UP Samantha Hunter
Forbidden Fantasies
Do you have a forbidden fantasy? Lauren Baker does. She's always wondered what it would be like to have sex with a total stranger. And now is the perfect time to indulge. After all, she's packed up her car and is on her way to a new life when she spots a sexy cowboy stranded by the side of the road. How can any girl resist?

#344 UNDERNEATH IT ALL Lori Borrill
Million Dollar Secrets, Bk. 2
Multimillion-dollar lottery winner Nicole Reavis has the world at her feet, but all she wants is hot Atlanta bachelor Devon Bradshaw. The Southern charmer has plenty to offer and plenty to teach Nicole about the finer things…including the route to his bedroom. But she's got a secret to keep!

www.eHarlequin.com

HBCNM0707